Time Doctors #2

Just in Time

Jacky Gray

To Paul - the best destroyer of words in the business.

Front cover design Copyright © 2022 GetCovers
https://getcovers.com/

Find out more at:
https://jroauthor.co.uk/
https://hengistpeoplehorse.blogspot.co.uk/
https://www.facebook.com/HengistPeopleOfTheHorse

Subscribe to Jacky's newsletter to find out the latest news and deals and receive your FREE Bonus Extras:
https://eepurl.com/b5ZScH

Contents

Prologue – The Dungeon

June 2022

"Roll up, roll up for the scariest show in town. Be prepared to have your hackles raised, your geese bumped and your timbers shivered." The jester character leered at a frail-looking woman, who stepped back as he got right up in her face.

"I think he got the pirate script by mistake," Kev whispered in Jen's ear, drawing the trickster's attention.

"What have we here? Fancy yourself as a bit of a critic, do we, sir? Or are you just hoping your lady friend will cuddle up to you at the frightening bits?" He jumped forward so sharply his forehead almost grazed Kev's, but he was expecting it and didn't flinch back, although he had no control over his blink reflex.

"Oohhh. A hard nut, eh? Novice mistake putting a target on your back, though – unless you're one of those who craves the attention. Got you pegged, Mr …?"

"You can call me Jinx."

"Among other things. A fellow trickster, eh?" He winked at Jen. "I would keep an eye on him, fair lady. Who knows what he'll get up to in these dark, cursed passages?"

The sound of bolts being drawn back drew his attention and he leapt up onto the low wall to address the small crowd gathered at the heavy wooden door. "Ladies, Gents, and those of you somewhere in-between" – he pointed at Kev – "welcome to our famous dungeon. This journey is not for the faint-hearted, so anyone who feels they might not be up to enduring the torments within, turn back now.

But don't expect a refund, you chose to pay knowing it would be the biggest fright of your life, it's clearly displayed everywhere around you." He picked on Isaac for a change. "Unless you can't read."

As Isaac prepared to give a lengthy discourse on exactly how brilliant a reader he was, the jester held up his hand.

"Don't bother to defend yourself; it's nothing to be ashamed of. Branson could barely read and look how well he did." He addressed the rest. "Seriously, guys, if you don't think you can take the pace, better to quit now, and I lied about the refund – you'll get it in full. Not so once you've entered this portal – even if you bug out in the first room."

The frail woman tugged on her companion's sleeve.

He peered at her. "Any takers? This is your last chance, folks. No? Well don't say you weren't warned."

He leapt down and ran through them, scattering those in his path, to open the metal-studded door and usher them inside.

Ch 1 – Awkward Decisions

June 2022

Jen glanced down at the square she'd been crocheting, and swore. "Bugger. How ready am I for the weekend?"

Ben glanced up from his kindle. "Problem?"

She held up two squares. "Just look at the state of that."

He peered at them. "They look fine – I'm guessing they're supposed to be the same size, right?"

"You would guess right, but the green one has two extra rows. I'm so wound up I got the tension far too tight."

"What are you knitting, anyway?"

"It's crochet. I had to give up knitting because Isaac whinged about the noise of the needles clacking. It's a baby blanket for Timmy's second, but at this rate he'll be all grown up before I finish it. Sorry for disturbing you."

As she removed the hook and pulled gently on the wool to unravel the last half hours' work, she realised her mind wasn't on the task. Not that her brother's new born would care if the squares weren't uniform copies, but the Virgo part of her strove for perfection. Which her mum said was why she was still on the shelf when Timmy got snapped up years ago despite being three years younger. But she knew that was more to do with his generous, caring nature.

Ben's chuckle drew her eye – he'd just downloaded Keith A Pearson's latest Clement book, always guaranteed to please. The irreverent anti-hero was a throwback to the seventies, when men were men and political correctness held no sway. She'd read a couple to see what the fuss was about and become hooked on the author's witty writing and memorable characters. The guy was probably as close to perfect as she'd ever found – Ben, that is, not Clement – but it was too late as her best friend Georgie had snagged him. Seeing the pair of them sprawled in identical positions on the two recliners raised a wry smile.

Jen found it strange how they'd all decided to make the early evenings a TV-free zone, especially Friday. A complete contrast to the pandemic when, to keep them from going insane, they'd binge-watched dozens of movie franchises and TV series. Now, they relished the peace and quiet to do nothing taxing. They certainly had the right place to do it – the beautifully decorated lounge overlooked the garden of what would probably be a mansion by most people's standards. A welcome breeze came in through the patio doors, relieving the heat of the warm evening where she chilled with three of her housemates. The fourth, Isaac – who was actually their landlord after inheriting the house when his Nan died – was absent. Frowning, she wondered for the nth time where he went on Fridays, but he refused to tell anyone, tapping his nose in that infuriating way he had.

Because she struggled to concentrate on anything cerebral, the crocheting occupied her hands. But the due date was creeping closer and she'd had little chance to do much in the past few weeks due to the insane hours they'd been doing at work. As they neared the release date of their current game, everyone lost their normal, laid-back disposition. *Who in their right mind would schedule a release a mere fortnight after the big Jubilee weekend?*

And if that wasn't enough, the past few months had been extra intense for her as she ran her own Dungeons and

4

Dragons campaign, *Tangled Warren*. Before that, she'd never realised quite how much effort Isaac put in to make every session run smoothly, and she was pretty sure Kev was finding it every bit as tricky as he prepared for their first session whenever the guy deigned to return.

The air filled with invectives as Kev cursed his displeasure, immediately apologising.

She glanced over. "Everything okay, mate?"

"Sure. Just another black hole I fell down half an hour ago. I wanted to get an overview for the next three or four sessions so I could mark them up on the map, but it led to nothing and now I've run out of time."

"How can I help?"

"I'd planned to print these off in colour, but the ink's run out and now they look naff."

"Ooh, a colouring-in job – just what I need."

"Sorry. I never meant to suggest–"

"Don't worry. I'm teasing." She stowed her bits in the cute knitting caddy Georgie had bought her, and ambled over to the table. "You know you don't have to go to all this detail – Isaac makes us work for stuff like this."

"True. You probably shouldn't see them, but I'm really struggling. It's a lot harder than he makes it look."

She grinned. "I just had that exact same thought, but remember he's been running campaigns for well over a decade. He could run DM masterclasses – or boot-camps."

He grinned. "That's much more his style. Trouble is, I struggle with his intransigence when it comes to disobeying rules. Our party in uni were a lot more flexible when the shit hit the fan. I'm trying for a compromise."

She squeezed his arm. "You do you, Kev – we're expecting nothing less. And you can be sure you'll know if we don't like it." A wink.

"*I'd* expect nothing less. Except, maybe give it a couple of sessions first? And be gentle with me?"

"In your dreams, pal."

~*~

Watching Jen fail to focus on her baby-blanket squares, Georgie couldn't believe she hadn't already discussed her recent adventure with her best friend. But Ben had been adamant about not telling the others yet. She hated hiding things, because she had anything but a poker face.

Normally, Georgie had a wealth of patience due to spending her working days out in nature, but even Job would have been hard pushed to deal with the agonies of trying to get a moment alone with her co-adventurer. Or more accurately, co-conspirator, because what they needed to do now was keep all mention of their bizarre journey a secret until they'd sorted out a few things. The very last thing they needed was someone as impulsive as Kev grabbing the magic dice and rolling them just for the hell of it. Or for Isaac to confiscate them as he'd done his grandfather's notebook containing many years of research.

She considered Ben's flippant suggestion that the only way to get a moment alone together was to buy into the rumour of a romantic attachment Kev was spreading. Something which, under normal circumstances, she'd shy away from – barge poles sprang to mind. *But needs must.*

Her chance came during Isaac's mysterious weekly absence when Kev called Jen over about his campaign. She put down her Jodi Picoult novel – the edges curled from so many re-reads. "Um, Ben. Have you got a minute or ten? Something's up with my laptop."

Kev glanced over. "Can't you get your power of thought woo-woo to fix it?" Her eye-roll had him changing his tune pronto. "I can help if you want."

"Thanks mate, but I've got this." After shutting Kev down with a frown, Ben beckoned her. "Bring it here."

Drat. This wasn't going to plan. "It's – um – about the battery life. I've just put it on charge in my room and I don't really want to unplug it until it's fully charged."

"Sure. Lead on."

Kev's eyebrows shot up and he nudged Jen who glanced up, rolling her eyes at him and shaking her head.

Trying to play it cool, Georgie felt her cheeks flaming at Kev's stage whisper. "I don't *think* that counts as trying to hide it – they must know we're onto them."

Ben echoed the eye-roll as they climbed the stairs. "Take no notice – he's got the original one-track mind."

She scoffed. "Don't I know it? But hopefully it'll mean we get a bit of peace." Leading him into her bedroom, she scanned the room to check she'd not left anything embarrassing lying around. But, as ever, it was neat as a pin – not a thing out of place. A remote part of her brain assessed this was the first time they'd been alone in her room since Kev decided they were an item. And certainly the first time since they were forced to share a room and she'd flirted enough to get him all hot and bothered to convince Isaac's gran of the very same thing.

As he pulled the door, she shook her head. "Leave it

open. We need to be aware of anyone skulking outside."

He grimaced. "I hate all this cloak and dagger stuff."

"Me too. But until we've had a chance to reflect on what went on, it's essential."

He took the wheelie chair at her desk, opening the lap top and clicking on the start button, glancing up as she dragged the stool over. "Might as well check this out while we talk – that is, if you want me too. I didn't mean to assume you can't do it yourself."

"Assume away. Mucking with computers leaves me cold. And it adds authenticity." She pulled the ribbon in her journal, opening it at a page full of notes.

"Blimey, you've been busy."

"It's been doing my head in. The only way to stop the thoughts going round and round when I'm trying to get to sleep is to write it down."

"Read me what you've got."

As she recapped their accidental leaps backward and forward in time, he whizzed through several screens on the laptop, occasionally clicking to change a setting.

He sat back when she finished. "So, in a nutshell, we found the cool room in the attic where Isaac's grandfather invented a time machine, but we can't ask him because he's AWOL or more correctly, MPD: missing, presumed dead."

A slight scoff. "We know it uses two dice which only seem to work if they land on the same number."

"Yep, and we had four separate journeys: first to 1977, where we met Isaac's Grampy Eric and his Nan, Naomi."

"And helped with a Silver Jubilee party." She grinned.

"Yep. But instead of returning here, we went to an

alternate 2022 where Isaac and Kev became chavs and Jen had a Stepford wives thing going on."

"Because I left a note in seventy-seven warning about the effect of Isaac's parents taking drugs." She grimaced.

"Don't beat yourself up. It all worked out in the end. We avoided the paradox when we returned to get rid of the note despite having two versions of me in the attic."

"Which meant next time you rolled the dice we got back to the correct timeline. Thank goodness."

"Amen to that. Rewind a bit – you mentioned when we went through the portal the first time you felt drunk?"

She nodded. "I bypassed pleasantly squiffy and went straight to barf and blackout."

He chuckled. "Sorry, I'm not laughing at your condition, I just love your imagery. And sorry for not noticing at the time and being more helpful."

She slid him a sideways glance. "I imagine you had your own trauma to deal with."

"Not the first couple of times, I got away relatively unscathed, just a slight dizziness when I stood."

"Lucky you." *No bitterness at all.*

"A bit different the third time, though." He shuddered.

Grimacing, she remembered her horror when she'd reached for his hand and he wasn't there. "I've been imagining all manner of dreadful ordeals." She couldn't help the note of reproach creeping into her voice. "Didn't help when you refused to talk about it."

A shrug. "I was trying to process it. Still am."

"Fair enough, I'll back off. By the way, did you examine the dice? You said you wanted to."

"And risk dropping them? If you remember, both times we went back to seventy-seven was after I dropped them."

"If you have to throw a double to activate them, maybe we should separate them."

"That's a great idea." He handed one over. "I'm hoping they'll only work in the attic, but you can't be too sure."

She pocketed it, pondering on where might be a safe place to store it. "I wonder if the same person has to throw – or drop – them, or if we could both–"

"Trust me, we need to find out a lot more before we start experimenting like that."

"Which means getting hold of Eric's notebook. But you reckon Isaac's hidden it somewhere."

"I'm not sure if he's *actually* hidden it – I'd never dream of looking through his things. I only spotted it because I had to grab a folder from his room and he'd left it on his desk."

"But he lied when he found it in the time capsule originally, and I wouldn't put it past him to have lied about it all being in code."

"I don't know about all of it, but certain bits were definitely unreadable, just pages of numbers. And the diary entry I read was extremely obscure, as though he didn't want anyone making the connection about time travel."

Georgie frowned. "It was funny seeing them in their thirties. Naomi didn't seem to have changed much, but the Eric I remember was at least a couple of decades older. Still quite fit and active and, as I said before, quite touchy-feely. But in a totally appropriate, grandfatherly way. As in lots of bear hugs." She blushed.

He grinned. "I'd chuck the shovel away before the hole gets much bigger."

Slapping his arm, she grimaced. "I dunno why, but I'm never far from a double entendre when you're around."

"Don't put that on me. Pure as the driven slush, me."

She giggled. "I bet Kev's plaguing Jen with questions. He'll be desperate to know what we're up to."

He snorted. "In his head, he knows exactly what."

"I'm guessing he'll use it as an excuse to chat her up."

"True." Another snort. "God knows he's spent enough years trying to get close."

Georgie knew of his repeated attempts, but no way would she break confidence by hinting at Jen's true feelings toward Kev. It wouldn't be fair to either of them, because Ben would feel honour-bound to tell his mate. She tried to steer him away. "So where do we go from here?"

He shrugged. "Apart from the notebook, the main source of information is the computer in the time capsule, but Isaac's got that sewn up pretty tight."

"Except he let us up there to borrow the clothes for the platinum jubilee party. Maybe if you told him about finding the keyring, he'd let us check the pockets on the clothes in all the racks for the other decades."

"Good in theory, but there never was any keyring, I made it up because I spotted the camera in the capsule and figured he may be watching us."

"Shit. What are you suggesting? That he installed a camera to spy on us?"

"Not necessarily. Eric could have put the camera in to record what happened in the capsule when he activated the

11

dice. It's what I'd do."

Grabbing his arm, she squeaked in her excitement. "Isaac spent months up there during the pandemic. Do you think he figured it out and took a few trips on his own?"

He raised his eyebrows. "This *is* Isaac we're talking about. D'you think if he'd discovered time-travel we wouldn't be hearing about it every which way till Friday?"

She giggled. "As if. You're right, though. No way would he keep such a thing to himself."

"But that doesn't mean he didn't spend every waking minute trying to crack the code."

"True. You guys reckon he has a planet-sized brain – how come he didn't work it out?"

"Not sure. I could be wrong, but I get the impression he didn't get on with Eric too well."

"What makes you say that?"

"Little things like the fact he never really talks about him. Yet he'll go on about his Nan forever and a day."

"Mostly because she thought the sun shone out of him. I don't think he disliked Eric, just maybe never got close, because he was only eleven when he left. After that, she clung on to Isaac for support." She shook her head. "It must have been awful, losing the love of your life."

The heavy thump of footsteps on the stairs preceded Kev's ostentatious throat clearing before he appeared in the doorway. "If you pair have finished, we'd like to get started on the first scene of *Cursed Castle*."

"We'll be right down." Ben stood, stretching, and Georgie couldn't help noticing his ripped body, cursing at Kev's leer and smutty laugh.

Ch 2 – A Right Royal Affair

Cursed Castle

    Peter Grenville (Ben) – an Oxford history professor

    The Jester (Kev) – Non-player character (guide)

    Evadne Whyte (Jen) – a paranormal investigator

    Kurt Klein (Isaac) – her partner-in-crime

    Rosalina (Georgie) – a gypsy spiritualist

Having furnished everyone with a pack, Kev gave them a moment to check through it. He hoped he'd managed to get the amount of information about right, but feared he may have gone a tad OTT. He watched as they exclaimed over the artwork on their individual maps, and leafed through the character bios based on what they'd discussed at the session zero planning meeting. He'd even included sample dialogue.

True to form, Isaac complained. "This isn't what we decided – I had no idea my character was German."

"I thought it would make him more interesting to play, but feel free to revert if you can't hack the accent."

He scoffed. "As if. But with all the characters being ordinary humans, I suppose there'll be no magic."

"Not as you perceive it, but you're dealing with ghosts so there's plenty of scope for paranormal activity. Think of *Ghostbusters*." Kev winked as the others displayed various reactions to Isaac's inevitable petulance.

Jen broke first. "Give him a break, Isaac. It's bloody hard being DM for the first time, and Kev's put a heck of a lot of work into this. I've watched a couple of *Britain's Got Ghosts* episodes and I intend to overact my butt off like that

13

woman does." She gave a flourish, then winked at Kev. "Seriously, mate. I'm hugely impressed – and not a little disturbed – that you spent so much time making up new rules so we could play a modern scenario. Must have taken you ages."

"That's just how I roll." Kev snickered, adding his own flourish to an exaggerated bow.

Ben chuckled. "From the little I've done, the setting dictates the characters and these are perfectly appropriate. I love the idea of a murder mystery for a change."

"Not a murder mystery." Kev deadpanned. "Although the body count's up there with the best of them."

"A detective story then. It'll be interesting to see how it pans out with the D&D rules."

Kev tutted. "Ah, those. You may … err … find them a little relaxed – no – let's say flexible."

Isaac snorted. "Non-existent, knowing you."

"You may *think* you do, but–"

"Shall we just suck it and see?" Georgie's blush said she regretted her choice as soon as the phrase was out.

Jen jumped in. "Yep, stop stalling and get on with it. And we have to refer to you as Jester, right?"

Kev grinned at the certainty she didn't want him filling the gap with something inappropriate "No, the jester is part of the management team and your guide around the castle. Call me narrator. But not DM or storyteller." He launched into the initial scene.

The esteemed Oxford professor knocked on the door to the gatehouse.

He jumped as Ben got straight into character, rapping

14

his knuckles on the table.

It creaked open, revealing a short, hunch-backed fellow dressed as a harlequin with red and gold diamonds patterning his one-piece costume, topped with a three-cornered hat festooned with bells.

Kev plopped the jingling hat on his head, adopting a creepy tone. "Good evening, Professor Grenville. The others await in the library, if you would follow me."

"I'd be delighted. Lead on my good fellow." Ben's clipped, upper-class accent was unrecognisable.

The strangely-dressed guide bowed low. "It is but a short walk." The narrator took over in a normal voice.

Picking up the professor's overnight bag, he shot out, marching so quickly the professor had to hustle to keep up with him. He had no time to appreciate the solidly-built stone walls of the keep or the beautifully maintained lawn in the courtyard as the chap entered an opening to a covered walkway which ended in stairs to the first floor.

"Steady on, my good man. Would you mind slowing down a little? I'm struggling to keep up with you." He hurried up the stairs, catching sight of the man's foot as it rounded the door, which slammed shut with a crash, leaving him in comparative darkness. He struggled to lift the stiff latch, hearing the jingle of bells as he finally opened the door.

Dashing down the walkway, he saw several rooms open for public viewing with notices requesting visitors stay behind the thick rope barriers. The first room displayed a splendid tableau of life-like waxwork figures amid sumptuous antique furniture, and he peered in, seeing no sign of his guide. "I say. This isn't funny. Where are you?"

As he moved, lights flickered and crackled as though some entity matched his progress and his hand reached for the back of his neck to calm the rising hackles. He peeked in each room long enough to establish a) the room wasn't a library, b) the jester hadn't entered one of them, and c) there were no living people.

Shadows playing across the faces of certain still figures caused their features to move in a manner guaranteed to unnerve, and he soon reached the limit of his tolerance to spooky situations. Every so often, he thought he heard a scuffle and twice shot a furtive glance backward before realising the bells would warn him of the man's movement.

A childish giggle was curtailed by a sharp smack, followed by tears and then a shrill shriek.

He jumped backwards, colliding with the hunchback, and the hat jingled, making him wonder how he could have appeared without a sound. "Where did you get to?" The sharp tone mixed fear, anger and frustration.

"This way." He offered no explanation as the narrator set the next scene.

The jester headed left, where a short corridor led to a taller-than-average door. He had no trouble opening it to reveal a library which would have swallowed the ground floor of an average English terraced house. The professor scanned the room and a cool blonde stepped forward, her hand outstretched.

"Professor Grenville. How good to finally meet you. I

hope your journey was … uneventful."

Jen had questioned Kev's original idea of her character being permanently excitable, suggesting it would add more scope for intrigue if that were merely her on-screen persona. He loved the way she hit the ground running, connecting with her character from the first scene.

His recent ordeal forgotten, Grenville bowed low over her hand. "Delighted, Miss Whyte. I'm sure you hear it all the time, but you look very … different in real life."

Evadne's cool gaze appraised him. "I wouldn't have put *England's Scariest* on your favourites list."

"Not normally, no." His candour should have rankled, but if it did, she made no sign of it as he continued, completely unaware of the slight. "But I watched a couple of shows after your assistant contacted me."

She tittered. "Kurt is a lot of things, including writer, director and producer." She gestured to the man whose glare could have boiled water. "Come and meet the professor, dear."

The narrator took up the tale.

The dour man, on whom a monocle would not have seemed out of place, took three steps forward, just stopping short of clicking his heels. "Guten tag, Herr Greville. Pleased to make your acquaintance."
But the lack of handshake suggested not.

Isaac's visible outrage at Kev's over-the-top typecasting threatened to break the mood, and Jen glared both of them into submission before picking up the – deliberate – error. "It's Grenville, Kurt. Greville was the name of one of the families who owned this castle. An easy mistake to make."

"You're correct. Forgive me, Herr Grenville." Isaac's German accent was even more authentic than Kev's.

The professor waved his hand airily. "Of course, Herr Klein. You're more than forgiven. I must say, I'm impressed by your grasp of the technical equipment required to prove the presence of paranormal activity."

The German film-maker sniffed. "Eva. I've set up the cameras and EMF gauges. We should–"

Ignoring him, Evadne gestured at the exotic creature hovering by the fireplace. "This is Rosalina, an extremely talented spiritualist we've used on several occasions."

The dark-haired girl bobbed her head. "Thanks, that's very kind." A shrug. "I've been given a gift, and I'm happy to use it to help. Can I get you some tea?"

The professor smiled at her. "That would be lovely, thank you. You're very kind. Are those biscuits I spy on the sideboard?"

"Of course. Help yourself."

The jester clapped his hands. "If you would take a seat, I have some vital information." When they were seated, he fixed them with a steely glare. "You may have heard stories about the dirty deeds attached to this castle, but I can assure you the reality is far worse than you could ever imagine." He shivered ostentatiously, his bells jingling.

Evadne leaned forward. "I've read a lot about the goings on in this castle with apparitions of slain noblemen and manifestations of nasty, vengeful spirits."

Professor Grenville nodded. "I've heard of disembodied voices and several shadowy figures being seen."

"Ja. I, too have heard about the orbs of light and sudden

temperature drops."

Holding up his hands, the jester explained their mission. "We have always been aware of these spirits who share our castle, but in the past few months, the nature of the activity has changed, as though something dark and sinister is disturbing what we think of as our friendly ghosts. It seems they are being subjected to an evil influence which makes them do things out of character."

"You mean the ghosts are being haunted?" Kurt smirked at his own wit, but no one responded.

"We fear this dark entity is growing in power and hope you will be able to identify him – or her – and discover what is causing this distress and how we can eliminate it. Do you accept the challenge?" He peered at them.

"I do." Evadne inclined her head.

"Ja. We shall seek and destroy." Kurt made a throat-slitting gesture.

The professor cleared his throat. "I'm not exactly sure how I can help, but I'll do my best."

"Your expertise in the history of this country and in particular this castle during medieval times will be invaluable."

A cough. "W-why thank you."

"And what about you?" The jester addressed Rosalina who had become very still.

"There is a presence in this room as we speak. Give me a moment–"

He clapped his hands. "I knew you'd sense her. While you're tuning in, or whatever it is you do, I must warn you all of the dangers of this mission. The owners of the castle are concerned about your safety, so you will not be allowed to roam around willy-nilly." A snigger. "Certain places have restricted entry, so it's important you don't go anywhere unless accompanied by a guide. Which for most of your excursions will be me." A hard look. "Are we all clear on that?"

As everyone else nodded, Rosalina's head shot up and she trembled, her eyes going out of focus.

"Here she is." The narrator pressed a button and strains of an old music hall Wurlitzer wrapped around them, with old-phonograph crackles accompanying the war-time warbling of "Daisy, Daisy, give me your answer, do."

Rosalina's voice transformed into a slightly nasal accent not unlike the Queen's. "I was born Frances Maynard in December 1861, but everyone called me Daisy. Why have you come to my home?"

"Lady Warwick, we are delighted to make your acquaintance and hope we will not cause too much of an intrusion." The professor gave a slight bow.

Evadne spoke up. "We've heard the castle is under attack from an evil entity and want to help rid you of it."

"I see." Her tone became guarded. "And what makes you think you will succeed where others have failed?"

Kurt straightened in his chair. "Because we are leading paranormal investigators using thermal cameras and the latest infrasound EVP detectors."

Rosalina frowned. "I have no idea what most of those words mean. And it's not simply your accent."

Evadne explained. "He means we have sophisticated equipment to monitor and analyse paranormal activity."

She gestured at Kurt, who hurried to fuss with the equipment.

"You mean ghostly spirits? If that's the case why not say so?" Rosalina stiffened. "I much prefer straight-talking people; they are more honest and trustworthy." She patted the professor's hand. "*You* may call me Daisy. How much of an intrusion remains to be seen, but if it means the end of these distressing episodes, it will have been worth it."

The obvious snub to the other two had them bristling with indignation. Evadne recovered quickly, sending an unspoken message for the professor to take the lead.

"Lady W … Daisy. Can you tell us more about the recent changes you have experienced?"

The guarded tone returned. "I often met a girl in the first flower of youth who roamed the grounds quite happily, particularly the peacock gardens. But now she trembles in the conservatory, too afraid to step foot outside it."

As she spoke, he scribbled in his notebook. "Go on."

"More distressing are the tears of a mother and child, but when I approach the source, their pitiful wails cease."

"That must be harrowing." He stopped writing, but Evadne made a note.

"Even more so because they are close to the foulest of …" She broke off, obviously upset.

Evadne tried to divert her. "Lady Warwick. If it's not too upsetting, could you tell us a little background so we can get an idea of your life in the castle? I heard Queen Victoria considered you as a possible wife for her son."

"Leopold?" A scoff. "It would never have worked, he was too frail." She declined to elaborate. "And my parents weren't exactly keen on Lord Brooke, despite his wealth."

Grenville nodded. "Ah, you mean Francis Greville."

Evadne tittered. "That must have made for some fun." Her snigger halted at the imperious glare. "What with you both having the same name and all. Ok, not quite the same – Frances and Francis–"

"Do you not listen, woman? I *said*, my preferred name was Daisy."

The professor tried to calm her down. "I believe you were both key members of the Marlborough House Set."

She relaxed back into her seat with a mischievous grin. "Those daredevils. They lived every day as though it might be their last. Speed was one of their primary goals, whether it was boats, automobiles or women."

He chortled. "The faster the better."

"Exactly. And Albert was the worst – and the best – of them." A secret smile.

"The Prince of Wales? I believe he was a regular guest here. Along with Winston Churchill." He'd seen the evidence in the wax models mere minutes ago.

Evadne seemed keen to steer the conversation down a different path. "You certainly lived a full life, but I heard of several scandals–"

"I don't wish to talk about them." With a hostile glare at the two investigators, she folded her arms and huffed, addressing the professor. "We haven't been formally introduced, but from what I've witnessed, those two are *not* the types I would invite into my home. *You*, however, are welcome to stay and I hope to meet you again."

"My humblest apologies, Daisy. I am Peter Grenville, a

history professor at–"

"Grenville, you say? Only one letter different. I wonder …" With a head-shake, she curtailed her musing. "I shall call you Pierre, because your obvious breeding speaks of a Norman heritage. But please, if you must have *them* in attendance, ensure they learn some manners."

"Thank you, and once again, my humblest apologies for the imposition. I assure you, my colleagues meant no offence – they are as keen to help as I."

She sniffed. "There are many other spirits, troubled and otherwise, residing here and few of them are unaffected by this malevolent ghoul. I will do what I can to aid your search, but be aware I have certain limitations."

Rosalina's head dropped down, her whole body stiffened, and then she rolled her shoulders, slowly raising her head. Blinking, she peered around the room, and Kurt adjusted the thermal camera to get a close-up image of her.

"Are you all right?" The professor poured a glass of water and offered it to her.

She took it, drinking gratefully, then pressed the glass to her forehead. "Thank you. It's quite … tiring, and takes me a while to recover. What did he say?"

Kurt glared at her. "You didn't even realise it was a woman? This is most irregular."

She shrugged. "I don't always know, particularly on the first time. The energy was quite … strident and confident. It felt like male energy."

Evadne glared at him. "Lay off her. She's probably feeling quite fragile and doesn't need the Spanish Inquisition–"

"Nobody needs that." The professor winked at her. "Or even the German one."

Kev gave himself a mental hug – this was going so much better than he'd ever imagined. They'd picked up the nuggets of information he'd suggested and everything was working well. He tuned back in to hear Evadne remonstrating with her producer that just because they'd had one fake psychic, it didn't mean they were all frauds.

Predictably, he stiffened, muttering darkly.

Evadne reached out to touch Rosalina's arm. "Take no notice of him, love. You did really well and we've all learnt so much thanks to your skill."

Blustering a protest, Kurt scanned around her body with the emf meter, noting down the readings.

Grenville glowered at him. "I think that's enough for tonight. Rosalina looks out on her feet and I don't know about the rest of you, but I would appreciate some supper."

The jester shook his head. "Of course, of course. We were supposed to dine before starting the investigation, but sometimes events conspire to overtake us. If you'd like to follow me to the dining room, I'll bring some tasty treats while cook prepares the meal."

Ch 3 – The Plot Thickens

June 2022

By the time the rest of them reached the kitchen, Kev had set out a couple of trays of canapes, and was opening a bottle of their favourite prosecco.

"Whoa, what's all this in aid of?" Ben nabbed one of the small circles of cream cheese wrapped in smoked salmon with a sprig of feathery dill, popping it into his mouth and letting the flavours and textures work their magic.

Sharing the last drops of sparkling wine between the five glasses, Kev grinned. "I thought I'd treat us, because it's my first one, and you've all put in the effort to make it work. Which I appreciate greatly."

"Mmm, this is so good. From the finest range?"

"Yep. Try a chip wrapped in bacon, they're to die for."

"Blimey, Kev this looks great, mate." Georgie clapped him on the back. "Any veggie ones?"

"All except aforementioned bacon. I think you'll like the chickpea and salsa, and the miniature pasties are beetroot and sweet potato."

Jen bit into one, nodding. "Good."

"I've phoned through our usual order at Wagamama. Should be here around half past. And it's on me."

"There's extravagant. Are you trying to butter us up so we'll give you good feedback?" Isaac took one of the chickpea canapes, sniffing and examining it.

"Only you, Isaac. Only you." Georgie shook her head.

"What? I'm just saying."

"You always, 'just say.' And it's never complimentary."

Jen wagged her finger at him.

"Why is everybody always picking on me?" He did his best Charlie Brown impersonation.

"Because you're such a jerk? Because you never have a good word to say about anything? Or anyone." Kev's resentment was showing.

"Do you two have to squabble over everything? It always sucks the joy out. Kev did a nice thing, Isaac. Instead of suspecting his motives, you could try and act grateful for once." Jen picked up a glass. "I'd like to propose a toast. To Kev. For a first-class first session, and especially for going an extra mile. This is fabulous, thank you." She raised the glass and clinked it with Kev's.

"You're very welcome. Thank you for helping to make it work. Although Georgie has to win the best actress award – that accent was cut glass."

"I'd have to give Isaac his due – the German one was spot on. No doubt courtesy of the war movies he devours."

Kev clinked his glass with Ben's. "You got *that* right. It worked even better than I could have hoped." He winked at Isaac. "You're a natural. So much comedy potential."

After they'd all taken a swig, Ben proposed a second toast. "To Kev's first DM sesh. And to the party. We rock."

After more clinking and swigging, Kev asked the question which had bothered him most. "Tell the truth guys. Did I overdo the info packs?"

"Yes. Dialogue suggestions are a no-no. And you say *I'm* patronising." Isaac scoffed.

"Um, for once, I agree. Although I didn't so much feel patronised as …" Ben was rarely stuck for a word.

"Babied? Mollycoddled?" Jen tried a couple.

"Overprotected is the closest I can come up with. As though you didn't quite trust us to get there on our own."

"In other words, patronised." Isaac sneered.

"Well I don't know about the rest of you, but I appreciated it." Georgie waved her glass in his direction. "Makes a nice change to have some of the research in front of you. Means you can choose what to use."

"Before the food arrives, I need to do your health checks." Isaac pulled out his digital thermometer and pointed it at Georgie's forehead, making a note on his iPad.

"Seriously? Can't it wait till after we've eaten?" Kev grumbled.

"I could, but then we'd have to do it for another week. No point collecting baseline data unless it's reasonably reliable, and the other readings were all before dinner."

"Whatever. Do me first, because I'll have to deal with the delivery any minute now." Kev held out his arm for the pressure sleeve.

"Thank you. It'll be interesting to see if a D&D session has an overall effect."

"Except you'd need to do it before and immediately after to determine that." Jen knew all about experiments.

"I know that–"

"Yeah, he did it before and after gym sessions for a few weeks till we told him where to go." Kev grinned.

"All good research, but once a day will do for now." Isaac wagged a finger. "You'll all thank me when I derive a baseline you can use to monitor your health. So far, I've learnt Ben and Jen have unusually low BP and Kevin runs a little hotter than most."

"Ha. Knew it. Hot stuff, me."

"But your blood pressure is several points above the rest of us. Too many fish suppers, maybe?"

"What? Show me." He peered at the tablet.

Isaac pulled it away. "All in good time. Fools and children shouldn't see things half finished."

"Say what? Did you just call me a fool?"

"Not necessarily." Isaac ducked out of his reach as Kev took a swipe, but he was saved as the doorbell rang and Kev ripped the Velcro fastening, throwing the thing down on the counter and stomping off.

He shouted after him. "But we may have to redo that when you've calmed down a bit."

As Kev showed him a middle finger, Georgie picked up the cuff, positioning it on her arm. "Isn't that fudging the figures? Mind you, who knows what normal is as far as Kev's concerned?"

Ben spluttered on his mouthful of prosecco. "Harsh but true. Me next."

"Got somewhere to be?" Isaac's eyes narrowed.

"Nothing I want to share."

Georgie's face puckered. "Too much information."

"Err, exactly how? It was no information at all, just your overactive imagination."

As they shared a positively conspiratorial grin, Jen glanced away, wondering again why she couldn't be happy for her two best friends in the world who'd obviously made a connection over the whole jubilee thing. Busying herself with getting the plates out of the cupboard, she tried hard not to think of all the chances she'd missed because of her relationship issues. And trust, abandonment and a dozen other problems she had where men were concerned. Ben was head and shoulders above the rest of the pack when it came to … just about everything. But there was no point crying over spilt milk, as her gran would say. Her breath hitched as she realised it was the first time she'd thought of her in ages.

"Jen. You're up. Quickly, the food's here." Isaac's tone left no room for refusal and she submitted to the just-short-of-painful squeezing of her upper arm, trying to think calming thoughts so he wouldn't have to re-do it as he had the last time because it had run nearly all the way to 200. But he'd positioned it badly and the tube had twisted – or some other bullshit.

"Perfect. Save me some of the noodles this time, guys, you know they're my favourites."

Suddenly, she didn't feel very hungry, but she put a bit of everything on her plate because Georgie watched her like a hawk after finding out about her brush with bulimia in her first year at uni. Just in case she didn't already have enough neuroses. But she'd learnt her lesson: poor body image was a killer – literally. Any time she was in danger of slipping back into toxic thought patterns, she had a number of strategies in her wellness toolkit, the most effective of which was doing something which brought her joy. Right now, she could think of nothing better than sharing a meal in good company, and a glass or two of wine wouldn't hurt – it was Friday, so not a school night.

"All right, Jen?" Of all the people to notice her wobble,

Isaac would be the last one she'd put money on.

She smiled at him. "Sure. Miles away."

"Somewhere nice?" Kev picked up on it.

Drat. Sympathetic attention was the last thing she needed. Sliding a sultry glance, she played him at his own cliché game. "That's for me to know and you to find out." Winding a stack of noodles around her fork, she paused before raising it to her mouth, to find him watching her intently. "Not an audience sport, Kev."

"Right. Sorry." He glanced at his plate, then reached out for a dumpling, but there was only one left. "Um, anyone want the last dumpling?"

"Yes, thank you." Isaac made no move to reach for it, obviously expecting Kev to snatch it away as soon as he did – an event which had happened many times in the past.

Several eyebrows rose around the table as Kev picked up the plate and deposited it on the table next to Isaac. "All yours, mate. Enjoy."

"That's very kind. Much appreciated." Isaac snaffled it as though still expecting a last-minute sabotage.

"Damn me. Anyone spot an alien pod growing in the greenhouse?" Georgie grinned.

"As in, *Invasion of the Body Snatchers*?" Ben chuckled. "Not me." They high-fived, and Jen's smile dimmed a little as she dipped her dumpling in the spicy sauce and nibbled.

"Very funny." Kev's mini-glare dissolved as he returned to his current passion. "So, is everyone up for another session tomorrow? I mean, we don't have to if you have a better offer, I just thought–"

"Sure, I'd be happy to." Isaac nodded. "If you give us a

clue about what's coming, I'd like to research up front."

Georgie leaned toward Ben, covering her mouth as she gave a classic stage-whisper. "Make it two pods."

Ignoring her, Isaac smiled at Jen. "If you're free, I had some thoughts about developing our characters."

"Er, sure. I have a few errands first thing. What time would people want to start?"

After some toing and froing, they settled on two o'clock, and Isaac badgered her about her errands until she held up her hands in submission. Truth be told, she merely wanted a bit of space for her normal Saturday meditation walk, but she knew she'd have no chance of finding any peace, if he found out. She wouldn't put it past him to tag along, and that would have the exact opposite effect.

The following day woke up grey and drizzly – not her favourite walking conditions at the best of times. As though to make up for his persistence yesterday, Isaac insisted on treating her to breakfast. They went to the local Spoons, where she had her favourite Eggs Royale – basically Eggs Benedict with smoked salmon instead of ham.

Thrilled with the idea of bottomless coffee, he ordered a plate of American pancakes to share for afters.

Scanning around the half-full room, she spotted a couple of tables littered with empty pint glasses, and nothing on earth could stop her from judging.

He gestured at a table where six burly blokes were tucking into fry-ups, the amount of food on their plates said they'd gone large with extra sides. "Can't you tell their bodies are temples?" He sniggered. "And who drinks beer

31

before lunch time?"

Ashamed at her own thoughts, Jen chided. "Not our place to judge. You've no idea of their lifestyle."

He scoffed. "You don't need forensic detection skills to know they're manual labourers. The lumberjack shirts over wife-beaters are a dead giveaway."

Her whole body cringed at his casual use of the offensive term, and he frowned.

"Did I get it wrong? That is the correct term for the white vests stretched over their beer-bellies, isn't it?"

She scanned around to see whether anyone had heard, but there was no reaction and she hissed a reply. "If you're in America in the fifties, maybe, but not over here. Never."

"Sorry, just trying to be down with the kids. I forgot your political-correctness. Or is it 'woke' these days?"

"I'm neither." She winced. "Just a person who believes in treating everyone with respect and not making remarks intended to insult or belittle someone based on their gender, ethnicity or physical appearance."

"Isn't that the very definition of woke?"

"Whatever. I'm not getting into an argument about your dodgy attitudes. Why did you really bring me here?"

He adopted the hurt little boy expression guaranteed to have the exact opposite effect he intended. "Can't I treat my favourite housemate to breakfast without an ulterior motive?"

She'd perfected the don't-mess-with-me glare, and it hadn't lost any of its efficacy as he sobered.

"I need your help."

"That goes without saying. What is it this time?"

"Have you noticed how Ben and Georgie are always huddled together these days?"

"No, I'm not going there." She held up her hands.

He blinked. "What do you mean?"

"If they choose to get together, it's none of our business, and the least we can do is give them some space."

"Get together? You mean as in having sex?" He shuddered.

She grinned. "I guess I can be grateful you didn't call it coitus."

He squirmed, holding up fingers in the shape of a cross. "Stop. That's … no. I didn't mean anything of the sort."

Shaking her head, she loaded her fork with muffin, salmon and egg, pausing before raising it to her lips. "Go on then. Explain. Or should I say, mansplain, because you know you will."

He wagged a finger at her. "Your baiting won't work today, too much is at stake." He went on to explain how he was concerned about the time capsule, especially after what Georgie had said about it being like a museum. "Remember when you and the others went through the clothes and games when we first found it?"

"Yeah, we were just trying to get a sense of what it was all about, but it soon became clear they were all sorted into the five decades from 1950s to 1990s."

"I don't suppose you took any sort of inventory?"

Pointing at her full mouth, she shook her head.

"Not even a photo of the clothes? I thought I saw something on your phone."

She tried to hasten her chewing, mindful that she'd

33

probably suffer later, but his intense stare put pressure on to swallow more quickly than she should. "That was later, when we borrowed some clothes for the themed week. I thought it would reduce the time we spent in the capsule if we had an idea of the choices."

"That sounds like something I might do. Very smart." Seeing her slight frown, he hastened to add, "And no less than I'd expect from you."

"Is there a purpose to this? I don't see what it has to do with Ben and Georgie." She sipped her coffee.

"I think some stuff has gone missing, and I thought a photo might refresh my memory." Having dropped the bombshell, he casually speared the last piece of sausage, and wiped the toast around his plate, catching up the remaining egg, before stuffing the whole lot in his mouth.

She took the opportunity to clear her plate, trying to formulate a question which wouldn't provoke him into a downright accusation of theft. But why would he think those two had done it? Why would he imagine any of them would take stuff from the room without asking? Unless … "Is this about the clothes we borrowed for the jubilee party? You know they returned them on the next Monday."

He jabbed his fork in her direction. "That's as maybe. But some of them didn't make it back into the racks. Like that fifties rah-rah skirt you wore."

"Well that's no biggie. I bet she put it in the wrong rack. It's an easy mistake to make."

He grunted. "We'll see. Anyway, I think it would be a good idea for us to make a proper inventory. Some of that stuff's quite valuable."

"If you just wanted my help, you only had to ask." She tutted. "No need to invent some great mystery."

He pushed his plate away and retrieved his iPad from his man-bag. "Anyway, I had an idea about this afternoon's session. Kevin was kind enough to give me a hint about the next scenes, so I've researched and I think we can make something of them so the whole session isn't so one-sided."

She nodded. "Good. I did feel like a bit of a spare part yesterday. I don't know where Georgie got her material from, but that Daisy character took over."

"Not just her, Ben too. Hence my conclusion they were in cahoots."

She frowned. "That doesn't sound like him. I wouldn't expect him to do anything underhand, he's so honest."

Sitting back, he regarded her through hooded eyes. "Because you're such an honest soul. I'm sure you'd change your mind if you knew what he'd done."

She tensed, frowning. "What do you mean?"

He glanced away, focussing on the table of men who were playing a noisy drinking game. When disgust had curled his lip as far as it would go, his attention returned to the iPad which had booted up and required a password to connect to the internet. "I created a folder – ah, here it is."

She'd seen this behaviour often enough to know the distraction technique was his way of dealing with anything too heavy, and let it go for now. It was one of the many ways she and the others had learnt to cope with his particular flavour of eccentricity. Leaning over, she concentrated on the research, figuring a way to use it.

~*~

35

Notes from a Foreign Country

The first thing I noticed was the way people dressed – they certainly had bags more style and flair. People took care over their appearance – the men wearing smart jackets, and the women matching shoes, handbags and even coats. Everyone wore hats, the women's neat and also matching, the men's doffed at every opportunity.

People were much friendlier, with strangers exchanging smiles and greetings, and they seemed to have all the time in the world to chat, showing genuine interest. The language wasn't exactly a barrier, but the accents were much clearer and more precise – none of the sloppy consonant dropping which made everyone sound lazy and/or careless.

Everywhere seemed cleaner, as though people cared about their environment, and I passed several women, dressed in flowered aprons and headscarves, kneeling down to scrub their front porch. With a cheery, "Good Morning," I raised my hat to every one of them, receiving a smile and wave in return.

The currency was different, of course, which was the main purpose of the morning's jaunt. I had some coins, which went surprisingly far, but needed to stock up on the notes for future trips. Thanks to a kind chap I had concise directions, and soon spotted the three golden balls signifying the requisite establishment.

The gentleman inside seemed unduly surprised by my unusual request, but was more than happy to accommodate, given the quality and value of the item, and the profit he would make if the conditions weren't met. He took great care in ensuring we both had identical copies of the agreement – going so far as getting his wife down to witness both signatures.

Furnished with a wallet full of the folding stuff, I set off to make the necessary purchases, treating myself to a delightful "cream tea" at a quaint tea-shop which would not have looked out of place on an episode of Downton Abbey. Marvellous stuff.

One of the trickiest items to track down was a suitable travelling case. I cannot express my delight at finding a familiar department store in the high street, where I crossed the remaining items from my list, giving thanks for my good fortune.

Suitably kitted out, I was able to embark on the real mission.

Ch 4 – Beauty and the Beast

Cursed Castle

Alice de Beauchamp (Rosalina) – Ghost

The narrator introduced the session.

After a day exploring the castle, the team of ghost hunters assembled in the restaurant where they were treated to the best the castle had to offer. During the meal, Professor Grenville attempted to regale them with details about the castle's many incarnations.

"In 914, Ethelfleda, daughter of Alfred the Great, saw the potential of the hill in the bend of a river as an easily defendable position and built a wooden fortress."

"I understand the first actual castle was built a hundred and fifty years later by William the Conqueror." Kurt's attempt at an engaging smile caused a hesitant nod.

"Not precisely, but close enough."

Evadne tapped her foot. "Do we really need to know in such accurate detail? We've all read the brochure: they replaced the wood with stone, and various Earls added a hotchpotch of towers. Whoop-de-doo."

The professor flinched from her abrasive tone. "Er, no. I merely thought you might find it entertaining."

"A bunch of dry, dusty dates and names? Puh-lease!"

"I thought it might be useful when spirits come through, to help discover exactly what is distressing him."

"Or her." Rosalina shivered. "I'm sensing an invisible presence nearby."

"A woman?" Professor Grenville perked up. "Could it be Daisy – I mean, the Countess?"

"I'm not sure yet. Keep talking." The girl smiled at him.

"Please, for the love of all that's holy, don't." Evadne glared at them. "We're supposed to be investigating, and all you two want to do is sit around trying to show how clever you are. That Daisy woman gave us some great clues yesterday and we should be off following up on them."

"I must caution you, Evadne, not to treat the spirits so rudely. I understand it makes for better viewing figures, but there is no need to be so disrespectful. Lady Brooke *was* the Countess of Warwick, but even if she weren't I would urge you to treat her with some courtesy."

Evadne rolled her eyes, but quashed the instinctive retort. "It's far too complicated – I thought she married Francis Greville, so why can't I call her Daisy Greville?"

"You could, if you refuse to use her titles, but I suspect we may lose some of her cooperation."

"Ja, Eva. Sometimes, meine liebchen, you can be a little – how can I put this? – over enthusiastic in your hunt for the truth." The German smiled into her eyes.

She held up her hands in defeat. "Sorry. You're right and I apologise if I offended anyone." She squeezed his arm. "I can always rely on you to rein me in, thank you."

"Bitte schön." Kurt patted her hand. "Anyway, as I was saying, we need the countess to be on our side if we are going to find this evil entity."

The jester glanced at them, his smile quizzical, before continuing, his bells tinkling as he nodded. "You're right, but the lovely Daisy isn't the only female ghost haunting this castle. There have been a number of strong women ruling over this castle, ever since William the Conqueror appointed Henry de Beaumont the 1st Earl of Warwick."

"And the de Beaumonts were earls of Warwick for many generations I believe." Kurt butted in. "Except most of them they were known locally as de Newburghs."

"Right." The professor pouted. "Your research skills do you credit, but most of this *is* in the brochure."

Evadne grumbled. "It would be much more helpful if we had some notice before each expedition so we could research properly. I've found a great website."

Brandishing a folder, the jester smirked. "It's all in the contract. We have to respect the current residents–"

"Meaning the family who live here." Rosalina scowled.

"Yes. And due to the various evening functions, we must limit your access to places with paying guests and where people are working so as not to disturb them."

"Would it be possible to interview some of the staff? Their experiences would be invaluable."

"Certainly not." A tut. "I mean, I doubt the management would allow it, given current policies. Is that all?"

She glanced at Kurt, who gave a reluctant nod as he set the camera rolling.

Grenville cleared his throat. "The castle has a history of strong links to royalty, taking a strategic position during many wars, more often than not at odds with whoever owned nearby Kenilworth castle."

The jester consulted his notes. "In 1264, King Henry III was threatened by Simon de Montfort, a local baron living at Kenilworth, while Warwick's 8th Earl, William Maudit, supported the king."

Rosalina stiffened in her chair, but Grenville didn't

notice as he read from his notebook. "Maudit was not the most effective of Earls – with his enemy only six miles away, you'd have thought he would have–"

"My husband was a good man." The shrill voice coming from Rosalina's lips startled them all.

"Alice de Segrave, I presume." Kurt got in quickly. "I am honoured to meet the granddaughter of such a famous man. Please believe my colleague meant no disrespect."

"Intended or not, he has no right speaking of things which don't concern him." Her voice calmed a little.

Grenville's outstretched hand implored. "Lady Warwi–"

"I prefer Countess. And don't bother apologising." She spun away, addressing Kurt. "And you, Sire. What do you know of Grandfather?"

"That he had King Henry's favour, and was so successful as constable of Tower of London, he rose to chief justiciar of England. A formidable man indeed."

"You have the better of me, Sire. I would know your name."

"My name is Kurt Klein, Countess."

"Frankish? Yes, I see you have their bearing."

"If it would not be too distressing, we would know of your treatment at the hands of the Earl of Leicester." Kurt mimicked her antiquated speech patterns.

"Simon de Montfort did not sully his hands." She scoffed. "He handed the despicable task over to the castle's governor, John Giffard. The mortifying incident would never have happened if my husband had followed father's advice about fortifying the northern wall where it meets the mound." With an angry sniff, she glared at the professor. "I

41

suppose you were partly correct, but I don't care to admit how ineffectual he could be when it came to important matters like the castle's defences."

Kurt passed her a glass of water and she took a sip before continuing. "The forces bombarded their way through the wall and overpowered the small guard left after William had sent so many forces to defend the king."

"I believe the north-eastern walls were slighted, so the castle should be of no strength to the king." The professor said gently.

"Whatever *that* means." Evadne spoke for the first time in a while, her displeasure at being ignored apparent.

"It means deliberately destroyed." Kurt smiled kindly.

"It was no cause for mirth." Alice's tone sharpened. "William and I were forced to watch our home being desecrated by these foul-mouthed blaggards; it was horrible. And if our humiliation were not complete, we were bound and bundled into a filthy farmer's cart, surrounded by leering guards and driven to Kenilworth Castle." She shuddered.

"It sounds dreadful." Evadne's sympathy was genuine.

"You cannot begin to imagine the horror of being pressed betwixt two sweat-drenched bodies, jostled and flung by every rut and puddle." She closed her eyes, her voice dimming to a whisper. "All the time imagining what might happen when we reached our destination."

The others exchanged concerned glances, but they could do or say nothing to lessen her obvious pain.

Her eyes sprang open, full of fury. "That black-hearted monster rode up on his horse, gloating he would offer another choice, if I would beg for mercy." She straightened in her chair. "But I refused to give him the satisfaction. When he cantered off, one of the men, more tender-hearted than the rest, whispered I had made the right choice. He was not offering a mount other than Shank's mare."

"You mean walking." The professor frowned.

She nodded. "Chained to the cart, no doubt, with villagers jeering as we struggled to climb Blacklow Hill."

"Dear Lady, I fear we have subjected you to even more torment, remembering this ordeal. Please suffer no more."

She brightened with the ghost of a smile. "Thank you for your consideration, Herr Klein, but I have given you the worst of it. When we reached Kenilworth, de Montfort treated us with due civility, holding us in a comfortable suite while he demanded the exorbitant ransom."

Kurt nodded. "Nineteen hundred marks, I believe."

She inclined her head. "It took my father a while to raise it, but he released us on the same day it was paid. After providing a sumptuous feast in our honour. He arranged an armed escort, lending us his best horses, but insisted we travel under cover of darkness."

The professor was first to understand the implication. "Because he wanted no witnesses to his generosity."

"You have the measure of him. He had scant need of the ransom, it was merely a military tactic. News of our violent seizure and public humiliation would have spread quickly."

"Striking fear into the hearts of King Henry and his followers. Anyone who could treat a lady so poorly–"

"Would be capable of so much more in combat." Her smile held genuine pleasure at his grasp. "His reputation from so many campaigns was already formidable, but this was the opposite of chivalry."

"You make him sound charismatic."

The words tumbled out almost involuntarily until she broke off. "He was married to the King's sister and their seven children were evidence of his virility. He–" A blush stained her cheek, and she reined it in. "What a complex man. On the one hand a champion of democracy, on the other, a persecutor of Jews in Leicester. But that's another story." The discreet flutter of her eyelid could have been taken for a wink.

With that, her tale was told and the Countess released Rosalina, who flopped back into her seat.

"What a tale." The professor beamed his admiration.

"Really? She got kidnapped and carted to a castle where she made sheep's eyes at a racist bully." Evadne's scorn held more than righteous contempt. Jealousy coarsened her tone, and three pairs of eyes glared their disapproval.

A cough brought Rosalina back to the room and several hands reached for her water glass, Kurt getting there first.

The jester seemed in a hurry to move them on, saying they had many more paths to travel. "For tonight, I suggest we convene in the courtyard in fifteen minutes."

Then he became Kev, suggesting they had a comfort break and shot out, followed by Ben and Georgie.

Isaac caught Jen's arm, waiting till the others were well out of earshot. "Not quite as we planned, but how good an actress are you? The line about sheep's eyes was genius. And your hostility toward me will keep them off balance."

"To be honest, it was no better than yesterday. I'm not

engaging with it. Too much history and not enough action. Although it suited your character down to the ground."

"Alright Miss Grumpy. But you're right, I do love the historical bits, and our research yesterday was very useful."

"For you maybe. But I can see this stable one being exactly the same, there's no part for me at all. Yet somehow, Ben and Georgie seem to be rocking it."

"I would suggest their characters yesterday had a real chemistry, as though they'd worked it all out together. And everything points to us meeting the Daisy character again, there's a lot more to her story."

"But you stole his thunder with the countess – charmed the pants off her." She giggled at his wince. "Oh my God, I've been around cliché-Kev for too long. I swear the phrase 'nose out of joint' ran through my head."

"I suspect you're tired; it's been a long day. Maybe we should end it for now and do some work on the next couple of scenes he proposed."

"If the others agree."

"Or the house will be empty tomorrow morning–"

"Aye, aye, what's this?" Kev actually nudged and winked. "You two plotting together while the house is empty? Should I worry about cupid going around shooting arrows and none of them heading in my direction?"

"As if." Ben followed him in. "Your one-track mind's working overtime."

Georgie wasn't far behind, and she slapped his arm. "Don't knock anything that takes the pressure off us."

Kev resumed his seat at the head of the table. "I don't want you pair complaining because you didn't have time for a pee. I told you fifteen minutes."

"And it's only been thirteen." Isaac smirked. "Actually, if you all agree, I'd like to request an adjournment."

Kev's head shot up. "Why?" He peered at Jen. "Because you're not enjoying it? I notice you're not doing much."

"Because so far it hasn't been what I'm expecting at all. I can't remember the last time anyone had to roll a dice. It's been much more like a murder mystery than a campaign."

He grimaced. "Is that no good? I thought you liked the ones we've been on."

"I did. But there've been no murders and scant mystery. Just some great acting and a whole bunch of history."

"What about the ghosts? Didn't they work?" His obvious agitation made her wish she hadn't said anything.

She shrugged. "Look, don't just go on my opinion. I just drew the short straw, character wise. Ask the others."

Ben echoed her shrug. "Maybe I'm not the best person to ask either, because I've landed yet another plum part."

Georgie nodded. "Me, too. I'm feeling awfully guilty after having the starring role in *Tangled Warren*. I love getting to play these wonderful women. Isaac?"

Kev glanced at him. "Go on, let me have both barrels."

"It's actually not like any other campaign I've ever done." Isaac hesitated.

"I knew it. I'm rubbish at Dungeon Master aren't I? Should we just end this and go onto the next one?"

"Let me finish. Different isn't always bad. I'm thoroughly enjoying researching these historical characters and having some fun playing them, although I'm not convinced about my main character, Kurt."

"A mixed review."

"But in terms of the rest of it – Jen's exactly right. It's not a D&D campaign in any sense of the word. I'm not feeling the danger or excitement of an adventure, and as for the quest?" A shrug. "Beats me."

"So if you had one of Craig's paddles, it would be a one, right?" He covered his eyes with a hand, peeking through the fingers.

"You're fishing, and because of that, you lose a point. A three – and that's me being generous, dah-ling." Isaac actually did a Craig Revel Horwood flounce.

Kev shook his head. "I'm surprised you even know who he is. Anyway, if you will indulge me, I have a tentative outline for a scenario which you haven't seen yet, but feels much more like the traditional ones we do. How about we start it and see where it takes us?"

Isaac looked at the others who all nodded their assent. He snorted. "I have no choice if it's four against one."

The narrator set the scene.

After the short break, the ghost hunters assembled in the courtyard, surrounded by several bags and flight cases of equipment. The jester challenged Evadne.

"So where are you taking us, Miss Whyte? I imagine you have several leads by now."

With an exaggerated sigh, she consulted her notebook. "So we have the young girl trembling in the conservatory, and the mother and baby crying, close to somewhere foul. The stables maybe? They must smell pretty obnoxious."

The professor glanced at Rosalina. "Anyone else coming through?" When she shook her head, he took charge. "So maybe we can find out more about these two leads. Narrator, what do we know about this mother and baby?" He rolled the dice.

"A mother and baby were rumoured to be entombed behind a stone wall." The narrator folded his arms.

"Is that it?" The professor frowned.

"Sorry, that's all you're getting with that roll. Evadne, would you like to roll for more information?"

"Not about them, as I believe Lady Warwick may be able to tell us more when she appears again. I'd like to know about the girl in the peacock gardens." But the dice landed on three, so the narrator shrugged, glancing at Kurt.

He made a thing of stroking his chin. "I think we should search the gardens for unusual readings. Maybe Rosalina will be able to make contact."

Having distributed the equipment between them, they followed the jester across the courtyard, through the northern gate spanned by two towers.

Evadne could tell the professor was desperate to spout more historical facts, but he couldn't walk and talk at the same time. She found it strange someone so young and fit-looking would struggle to keep up with the rest of them, but kept the thought to herself.

Kurt was in his element, ordering people around until he had every piece of equipment set up to his satisfaction. The jester hopped around getting in his way, turning carefully coiled cables into knitting and constantly reminding how it would be getting dark soon. When they finally had everything ready, Kurt and Evadne scurried around trying to start everything simultaneously.

Rosalina remarked to nobody in particular they could do with a clapperboard like on a film set.

He shrugged. "It doesn't need to be *that* precise, but if they have a similar start time, it's easier to cross reference."

She glared at him. "How much easier would it be if you showed the professor and I what to do? We're not stupid."

"Please forgive me for giving that impression. I would be honoured to show you." As he demonstrated the emf detector, probably the easiest, Evadne showed the professor the basics of the instrument which recorded temperature, pressure and humidity, plotting the data on a graph.

The narrator rolled the dice on Kurt's behalf, informing him the equipment failed to detect anything.

He tutted. "There's no point sticking around here, then. It's always trickier detecting anything outside."

The professor nodded. "Of course, because all the signals will disperse into the air. Whereas inside, they will intensify as they bounce off the walls."

"So I suggest we move the equipment to the conservatory and set it up there." Kurt seemed a little less reluctant to accept help in packing things away, and Rosalina suggested it might be easier if he had a trolley to transport the heavier items.

"I have one, but one of the wheels jammed so it is impossible to push over these gritted paths." As he spoke, a mournful wail sounded in the distance. "What was that?"

Rosalina's eyes narrowed. "Maybe an animal in pain."

"It didn't sound like a wounded animal." Kurt shrugged. "Maybe one of the horses is giving birth."

"They wouldn't joust with pregnant mares." The

professor scoffed. "I thought it sounded more like a cow than a horse. Or a deer, if they are still kept here."

The wailing intensified, definitely louder.

"Whatever it is, I'm not sticking around to find out." Evadne picked up a flight case and rucksack. "Which way's that conservatory?"

Rosalina cocked her head. "I think it may be trapped – we should try to rescue it." Her features froze at the bellow coming from somewhere close.

"Run, everyone. Run for your lives." The jester once again showed surprising speed, given his impediment, and the crash of a large beast crashing through undergrowth had them all following him at speed.

The ground shuddered as the creature galloped behind, each stomping foot gaining on them as it bellowed in rage. None of them dared look back as they felt hot breath warm their backs, and Evadne reached the mostly glass building to find the front entrance locked. Shouting in frustration, she yanked on the handles, but they refused to budge.

"Go … round … back." The jester panted the words and she darted to the left, only to see him running towards the right, followed by the others.

Not wanting to risk drawing attention to herself by chasing them, she continued on. After rounding the second corner, she saw no sign – they should be running towards her, but she ran along the length of the building without meeting them. Panting, she shone the torch inside, wondering if they'd discovered an open door, again drawing a blank. They had simply disappeared.

The galloping hooves closed in …

"Sorry folks, that's as far as I got." Kev's statement was met by groans. "We'll have to pick it up next week."

"Always assuming the release doesn't have us in all weekend like last time." Jen pouted.

"True. Fingers crossed." Ben held up crossed fingers. "Much better, mate – felt more like one of Isaac's."

"Steady on – I wouldn't go that far." Isaac huffed.

~*~

More Notes from a Foreign Country

Nothing could have prepared me for the actual experience of travelling to this new place. I'd done my homework, researched everything I could – given the obvious limitations – but even so. What a truly delightful experience.

A friend of mine is smitten with everything to do with it, from the colourful – if a little zany – fashions to a culture where the youth are desperate to break free from the old-fashioned strictures of previous generations.

Whereas I wouldn't feel at home here, I can see the appeal for people who are so clearly bound to nature and the ideas of peace and harmony.

Yet again, there are problems with obtaining the necessary currency, but I discovered the rules on gambling are more relaxed and, for someone with an aptitude for numbers and research, there are ways and means of turning a small number of coins into sufficient notes to meet quite modest needs.

One of the most strikingly different aspects compared to my experience are the laws regarding transport. The attitude to road safety here is far more lenient with very little regard paid to protection in terms of mandatory seat-belt or helmet wearing, speed limits and the fitness of vehicles for purpose.

In fact, you could say this applies to almost every aspect of life here – they're not governed by rules limiting their freedom to do and say what pleases them. Nor indeed by rules – or rather social moirés – concerning acceptable behaviours, such as smoking, and attitudes such as sexual harassment and chauvinism bordering on misogyny.

But, as they say, when in Rome – not that I'm giving a hint in any way – one should do as Romans do. Although it is a tad tricky to fit in with these rather extreme outlooks after so many decades of indoctrination about what is and isn't acceptable to the great unwashed. The closest I can give you is watching the ground-breaking British drama series Life on Mars. *Oops – have I given too much away?*

Ch 5 – Release Crunch

June 2022

The next fortnight had all hands on deck at work as the four who worked for Gaming UK got roped into helping with the fallout from the release they'd all been working on for a while. Almost every night saw them still at the office at ten pm, and starting the next day at seven am. For the first week, the company laid on cooked meals throughout the day to suit all the weird shifts people were doing.

It got old quickly for Ben, but Kev raved about the nearly-all-day breakfast bar worthy of a posh hotel, which went from around five am until lunch began at twelve. Hot lunches were limited to a couple of hours, but salads and sandwiches were available for the rest of the day for anyone who missed out. More hot meals were served from six till eight, and by then, even Ben saw the sense of not having to go home and start preparing food. And the nominal prices made it too good an offer to refuse.

By the time they got home, the gang were all wiped out and everyone stumbled straight to their rooms, to do it all again in less than eight hours.

On the fourth night, Ben noticed Georgie's resignation as Jen and Isaac barely said more than hello before going to bed, and Kev secreted himself in the games room for a "half-hour blast." Realising they'd barely said a word since Kev interrupted them in her bedroom, he filled two glasses with ice and fetched the whisky, offering her a nightcap,

"Go on, then. A small one. Don't you need sleep, too?"

"This'll help me sleep." He poured the amber liquid,

handed her a glass and they toasted to a "straightforward release." Sipping, he relished the smokiness with a grin. "I was gonna say smooth release, but that had unsavoury connotations. Same with easy and pain-free."

"Sorry, what?" She squirmed. "Don't bother. Doubtless scatological, as Isaac would say. Don't need those images."

"So, how have you been keeping while we're all nose to the grindstone? It must have been lonely, rattling around the house on your own in the long evenings."

"Actually, I enjoy the peace and quiet. And anyway, I've been busy. With everyone gone, I snuck in some trips to the time capsule on my own. With only me in there, I managed a couple of dust-free hours. The first time, I carried on with the inventory of all the toys and games he's been nagging us to do."

"Bad luck, that must have been boring."

"You might think so, but I took a bunch of pictures to make it easier, then I sat at the computer and filled in a page of entries to keep him happy. But the camera isn't pointing at the screen, so I spent most of the time trawling through the folders to see if I could find anything."

"Clever girl. But I doubt he'd leave anything useful on it, because it isn't password protected."

"Who, Eric or Isaac?"

He shrugged. "The twinkle in your eye says you found something."

"Not until tonight. As Isaac hinted, Eric was fond of a code or two, but these were hidden in plain sight." She reached for her glass and sipped, her eyes sparkling as she obviously relished the chance to build up some intrigue.

Enjoying the moment, he curbed his curiosity and followed suit, settling back in his seat as he sipped, awaiting her pleasure with feigned unconcern.

"Pah. You know me too well. Not nice to steal a girl's thunder. In a folder labelled 'to be sorted and chucked,' I found a file called 'boring legal stuff, but as I scrolled down, under a load of guff about the house, I discovered the initial log he'd created. I read what looked like a diary entry. It was just like you said; he'd cleverly made it sound like a journey to a foreign country."

A snort. "The clue was in the title. But we know he was travelling in time. I wonder if he went forwards or backwards?"

"Something tells me the account I saw was not far in the past, but I only skip read it because her nibs was nagging at me to vacate pronto."

"Her nibs?"

"The computer."

"Of course. I got that, just questioning the phrase. I'm guessing your gran?"

"Yep, she spent a while up north where it was common. It means 'a person who thinks they're important.' Or something similar."

"I'll be borrowing that!"

The smile barely touched her lips, and went nowhere near her eyes as she swirled the liquid in the glass, the ice cubes jingling. "What do you think happened to Eric?"

He took a sip to give himself thinking time as he formulated a reply. "Honestly I had no clue, because I never met the older version of him. But from the few times

Isaac referred to him, I always thought he upped and left, leaving Naomi to carry the can."

"Pretty much the story we all got."

"But having met the younger version, I find it extremely hard to believe. That man loved the bones of Naomi, and he was no philandering quitter."

"You got all that after a couple of days?"

"Absolutely. He had a fierce loyalty to his family – you saw how he was with that wastrel of a son of his."

She grinned. "Your Professor Grenville is showing."

"Actually it's Alex who spoke in ancient tongue."

Her face dulled with concern. "Do you think Naomi knew about his time travelling?"

Ben shrugged. "A tough one to call. She must have wondered about his obsession with the attic, but whether she figured it out is another matter entirely."

"I suspect he tried to pass it off as a living museum the way Isaac tried to. All that stuff in dust-proof containers kinda backs it up, although it seems a strange hobby."

Ben grunted. "Trust me, blokes have far weirder preoccupations. And collections." He sipped. "I reckon we should get a copy of that file – and anything else on there. I never thought to look for a USB port – it would only take a few minutes to transfer it to a memory stick."

"Did they even have USB back then? It looks ancient."

"If not, I'll get an adapter to connect to a serial port – I used to have one, but I reckon it went the way of all flesh."

She grinned. "I looked for email but it wasn't obvious."

"I've no idea if Outlook even existed back then. You could always take a photo of the screen, but make it look as though you're just checking something on your phone."

"Of course. The camera's always watching."

"Talking of cameras, what did you think of their performance last week?"

Georgie relaxed. "It was cool that Jen got to have a proper go. She does a mean mean-girl. Very credible."

"I was thinking more about Isaac sucking up to the countess. I never expected him to go off script like that – he was always a stickler for the rules."

"It's fine by me – it's hard to break rules when there aren't any. And, as I said, plum role. I really wasn't relishing the stable boy – he's very …"

"Uncouth?"

"I was thinking laddish, but yes, uncouth does it better. And the danger made it exciting, like a normal session."

"Did you notice how much extra stuff Isaac added in? He and Jen must have been at it for hours."

"Did I hear that right?" Kev's appearance made them jump as he intended. "I knew it. I saw the way he was all over her at the start of the session." He mimicked a German accent. "Sometimes, meine liebchen, you suck. And did you know he bought her breakfast on Saturday? I reckon we'll be reading the banns by the end of the summer."

"Hardly." Georgie scoffed. "They were simply going over the script for the afternoon. She told me."

"Is that what they call it? As if." He mimicked an American teen. "Jen and Isaac, sitting in a tree. K-i-s–"

"Stop it." Georgie jumped up and ran out.

Ben rolled his eyes. "You really have to get some new material. That got old very quickly."

"And you and Georgie having a cosy nightcap? I bet there'll be more tiptoeing between rooms tonight than an Ayckbourn farce."

"Those are some mighty green eyes, mate. Will you be ripping your shirt off next?"

"Don't make me angry. You wouldn't like me when I'm angry." Kev flexed his muscles, Hulk-style.

"Whatever. I need sleep, man."

"Can you spare me a moment?"

Ben interrogated his glass which still had a few millimetres left, although it was probably 90% water. "Ah, what the heck. What do you need?"

Kev plonked himself down and grabbed the bottle, splashing a generous measure in Ben's glass, then grabbing Georgie's glass and half-filling it, his tone defensive. "What? I'm being green – less washing up. Georgie would approve. I can't imagine she has anything contagious."

Ben held out a hand, palm facing his bratty mate. "Not judging in any way, mate."

He winked. "And if she has, you'd have caught it by now and you're still standing." He took a long swig.

Ben refused to rise to the bait. "I'm guessing this is about your campaign. You want to know what I really think, without the others around to criticise my opinion."

"Got it in one."

"Honestly? I'm thoroughly enjoying the freedom of it. There are times it gets more than a tad tedious having to abide by Isaac's strict adherence to the rule book."

"A tad tedious?" Kev grinned, raising his glass. "As ever, you're being nauseatingly generous. He's a bloody control freak, and there have been times I just want to tip the table over and stomp out."

"Still? I'd have said that at the start, but you've seemed a lot less fraught recently."

"Because he's backed off a bit. Unless I'm imagining it, and it's purely that I'm making allowances for his quirks."

"Quirks? You're not normally that tolerant."

"Blame the girls. They have me brainwashed. I'm not allowed to call him autistic, or hint he may be anywhere *near* the spectrum, let alone on it." He heaved a sigh. "So, the lack of rules is a big tick for you?"

"Georgie, too. She's never known anything but rigidity from DMs, and she enjoys the freedom."

Kev's eyebrows shot up. "Rigidity? You surprise me."

"Inflexibility, then. Intransigence. Dogmatism."

"Rigidity AND Dogging? And you reckon I'm the one with the one-track mind."

Ben shook his head – there was no distracting the guy in this mood. Didn't stop him from trying, though. "Anyway, I told her about the party we had at uni – how it was much more of a party in every sense of the word."

A grin. "We were bad buggers back then, eh Benji?"

"Truly bad." His features turned wolfish. "Good times."

"Is that it? No more feedback?"

"Nothing that hasn't been said already, except …"

"Go on."

"Just that Georgie and I had a lot of fun preparing those scenes – we actually wrote bits of scripts and it felt much more like we were learning parts for an am-dram production than a D&D session. Although we didn't stick to them rigidly on the day." *Ba-ad word choice.*

"You're having a hard time staying away from boners today – when are you going to admit you and she are at it?"

"Doesn't matter what I say, you're gonna spread it anyway."

He exploded, jumping so violently he nearly wasted the scotch. "There's a whole psychobabble about how people inadvertently choose words related to whatever's at the forefront of their mind. You've got it bad, mate."

"If that were true, every other word out of your mouth would have a dick in it."

"Stop. You're killing me. I need to get outta here before my sides actually split."

As he wobbled off, Ben tried the idea on for size. Him and Georgie? *Surely not.* The chemistry was between the characters, not the players – *wasn't it*? Although he *had* found himself researching Daisy so Grenville could delve deeper. And there had been moments in the midst of Jen's campaign when he felt it was Georgie smiling at him rather than Sapphire at Avrin. *Pah!* It was just because they were playing characters who were romantically linked.

He shooed the images out of his head, but his brain immediately replaced them with scenes from their 1977 adventure where they'd actually shared a bed! Not in *that* way: she'd been fast asleep when he went up, and there was not so much as an errant toe touching as they slept. His poor, tired brain couldn't cope with the potential ramifications, so he went up to bed.

~*~

The following Tuesday saw the biggest rail strike since

1989 and, between that and Covid, none of the customer-facing team made it in. Isaac and Jen found themselves giving technical support to the online helpline together. As it went through a mid-afternoon lull, they happily agreed to man the chat bots while the two clerical staff who'd been covering went for an extremely late lunch.

Isaac wasted no time in turning the conversation to Georgie and Ben, asking if she'd noticed something going on between them.

She rolled her eyes. "Not you, too. I'm fed up with Kev casting aspersions about them – I promise you neither of them enjoys his constant razzing."

"No. Although it's possible the connection between Daisy and Grenville went deeper than the characters. But they do seem to be huddled away together at every opportunity."

"Because they're enjoying the opportunity for some real acting. I'm sure they're thinking the same thing about you and I." She checked the screen as the familiar beeps indicated a customer, but the bot handled the query easily. With a frown, she had an insight. "Is this because they stopped letting you take their temperatures? Those health checks got old very quickly – you said you'd only need to do it for a week."

"I would normally, but I noticed some anomalous readings–"

"Are you surprised? We've been working sixteen-hour days and stuffing ourselves with calorie-laden fatty stuff with virtually no exercise. Anyone would see that's bound to have an effect."

"Georgie hasn't been."

She narrowed her eyes. "What are you getting at?"

"I just found out she spent several hours in the time capsule while we were all at work."

"Doing that inventory you've been nagging us about. You can't have it both ways."

He held up his hands. "Of course. I'm just concerned about her. What would happen if she fell asleep or something and the machine started its evacuation routine?"

"Well she obviously didn't because she was watching TV whenever we got back."

"No, you're right. Take no notice – I simply worry because she's the only family I have left."

The chattering of bots on four of the screens drew their attention, and they didn't get another opportunity to talk. His suspicions burrowed into her brain and, without consciously trying, she found herself taking notice of their interactions. But it just felt like the Georgie and Ben she knew and loved, so she dismissed Isaac's misgivings as some kind of cry for sympathy – any darker motivation didn't bear thinking about.

On the Friday, she finally got a clue to the mystery of where he disappeared to after work. When they got the official notice that all the major fire-fighting was over, the company held an impromptu wrap party at three o'clock with a champagne – or at least, prosecco – fountain and some exotic nibbles in the dining room.

Jen clinked glasses with Isaac, watching as he took a tiny sip and put the glass down. "No good?"

"I'm – er – not feeling it."

"Do what? I know you're not the world's biggest drinker, but we've earnt this." She handed him the glass, toasting, "To us, and our heroic efforts."

He raised the glass, taking an even smaller sip.

"Blimey, mate. It's not as if you're driving or anything." It was a bone of contention that, like Sheldon, he preferred to be chauffeured everywhere.

"As if." He snorted, managing to spill the fizz over his hand. "Oh dear." Putting it down, he shot off, just as the other guys came up.

"What did he spill?"

"Guess." She held up her glass.

"Wastrel." Kev scoffed. "All the more for the rest of us. Good old Gaming UK." Another gulp and his glass was empty so he grabbed Isaac's. "What? He can always get another one."

Shaking her head, she forgot about it as the director came up to personally thank each one of them.

A short while later, on her way to the loo, she glanced out of the window at a red escort with a popular driving school logo on the roof. As she watched, Isaac got in the driver's side and, moments later, the car drove away. She hugged herself, promising to choose her moment for maximum tease-value.

~*~

Adventures in a Foreign Country

Although this is not my first foray into this particular locale, each trip brings with it certain hazards. This entire project has helped me discover a talent for espionage I never dreamed I'd have, no matter how many black-and-white gumshoe films I watched.

My first mission was to gather as much information as possible on the targets. I was aided and abetted by several helpful souls, in particular a certain landlady. I could never see it happening in my world because my neighbourhood is anything but neighbourly. Everyone keeps to themselves, and people have no clue who they've lived next to for the past decade. I'm sure my street has its own curtain-twitching busybody, but I've yet to meet her – or him!

"Are you lost, dearie? Can I direct you somewhere?"

"That's very kind, but I'm just enjoying this beautiful day and the peace and quiet."

"Oh, I'm terribly sorry. I didn't mean to disturb you."

"I'm not disturbed at all and grateful for your kind concern."

"We're a friendly neighbourhood and, after the war, we all like to look out for each other."

"Of course. Highly commendable." Just the right amount of clipped, military tone. "We certainly would never have made it through without all you lovely ladies doing your bit."

"You're too kind, sir."

Her reluctance to move on suggested loneliness, and her smart clothes and laden shopping basket said she fitted my bill exactly. I had to find exactly the right level of insouciance. "I don't suppose you could recommend a guest house around here? My fiancée *gave me the details but I seem to have lost the note."*

That apparently, was exactly right, resulting in an invitation to share her elevenses – which meant the ubiquitous pot of tea and plate of homemade cakes. With my credentials established, she leaked information like a rusty sieve, the most valuable being a certain phone number.

My detection skills were barely required to find the department store. I managed to procure the exact item despite the assistant's insistence my fictitious fiancée – who was coming in handy – would prefer a more frivolous styling. I still had more tasks – one in particular I was not looking forward to – but they needed to wait for a subsequent jaunt.

Ch 6 – Day Trip

June 2022

After the full-on weeks, the company treated them all to Merlin tickets, which seemed like a sign, because it meant a free trip to Warwick Castle. Kev had been keen to go after a visit had inspired his D&D setting, but hadn't managed to get them there due to distance and steep admission. He was proper thrilled about the adventure.

"This is great." He nudged Ben. "Remember Jack from uni? He works in the dungeon and can get a Merlin pass so Georgie can get in for free too. Sorted."

Ben didn't want to sound all parade-rainy, but he'd just been doing the math. "I'm bloomin' glad I've not needed the car this month. Last time I filled up it was just over fifty-five quid, but with Monday's hike in fuel prices, it'll be closer to sixty-five. The journey there and back will be at least three quarters of a tank with five in the car."

"Still cheaper than going by train." Georgie winked.

"Chance would be a fine thing with all the strikes they're on about – deliberately picking Saturdays to hurt people in their free time." Jen scowled, thinking of her mate's brother. "After so many postponements over lockdown, people have finally planned their dream weddings. And now some of their guests will struggle to get there because of militant rail workers."

Kev frowned, trying to regain the mood. "Don't worry, Ben. We'll all bung you a tenner towards the petrol. I can't wait to see what you guys think of Jack – he makes a brilliant jester – taught me everything I know."

They made a complete day of it, starting early to avoid the traffic, and Kev knew all the insider info about parking near the stable entrance to avoid the long walk, and booking early for the dungeon tour to avoid missing out – the good weather brought people out in droves. He'd even given them a list of all the "don't miss" attractions and the ones to avoid "like the plague." He'd suggested booking an evening table in a restaurant on the high street, as getting fed in the castle meant long queues and nowhere to sit, so they took some butties to keep them going till dinner.

The highlight had to be the dungeon tour, and they got to see Jack in action. Jen thought it was a bit unfair because Kev knew the routine, and he'd obviously pointed Isaac out so he got picked on unmercifully – and not just by the jester. The plague doctor chose him to demonstrate on, the executioner locked him up in a cage, and the judge heckled him at every opportunity.

Each of the characters managed to impart a bunch of historical information without making it sound dry and dusty. The torturer, played by a tall, imposing woman, explained how many prisoners were held in Caesar's and Guy's Towers, and their ghostly cries at the hands of her predecessor could still be heard. People jumped as ghostly wails echoed around the chamber. With a wolfish leer as some people reacted, she continued.

"During the Civil War in 1642, a certain Edward Disney was locked up in Warwick Castle dungeon after the Battle of Edgehill. The Earl of Warwick at that time, Robert Greville, supported Cromwell."

Isaac nudged Jen. "What's the betting Kev will have *that* scene in his cursed castle?"

The tall woman glared at the interruption, inviting him to sample some of her work. He declined, zipping his lip.

An absolute professional, she didn't miss a beat. "Disney was fighting for King Charles I, and we know about him because he doodled some graffiti on the wall of the dungeon. No doubt the artistic streak ran in the family." She grinned. "The story reached the ears of the great Walt Disney himself. He obviously thought it possible they were related because he came to the Midlands in the 1940s to try and trace his family who he believed formed the village of Norton Disney not far from here."

Jen liked to think of herself as made from stern stuff – the times when she would jump at shadows for days after watching a scary horror movie were long gone. Mostly, she was in awe of the phenomenal performances from all the actors. Kev mentioned that most of them played D&D – no surprises there, then – and speculated how awesome it would be to play a session with them.

A couple of times, the special effects caught her unawares, and her analytical brain immediately got on the case to figure how they'd managed to convince people a plague of rats were running amongst them as they sat on wooden benches. Inevitably, Jen got picked on, also by the judge, who had her hauled into the dock, where he accused her of all manner of crimes, mostly involving corrupting the morals of her poor innocent serving lads.

But the one making the most impression was the almoner, played by a tall, slender girl whose beauty shone through the drab costume, her blonde curls escaping the unflattering cap. Aided by several special effects, she'd made everyone in the room jump when the lights extinguished. Moll Bloxham, the witch who'd been the subject of the almoner's tale, tore around the room, screeching at people.

After an excellent dinner, Ben drove them home with everyone but her snoring.

~*~

The following week saw the start of Wimbledon, and Jen morphed into a complete fan-girl, recording all the day's play and wanting to catch up every evening. As usual, she'd booked the second week off as holiday, and had tickets to watch it live, and it seemed the only time the others saw her was if they happened to be making food the same time she grabbed a snack.

Kev pretended to pout. "So that's it. We won't be able to carry on with *Cursed Castle* till you come back to us."

Isaac groaned. "Really? We've already had to leave that cliff hanging for a fortnight and now another one."

Seeing her stiffen, Ben tried to take some heat out. "Will you be staying with your cousin in Wimbledon like last year? So good to have friends in all the right places."

"What's that supposed to mean? Why don't you lot stop trying to make me feel bad about wanting to follow my passion? I'm sure you can carry on without Evadne – she had virtually nothing to do in the first few scenes, and anyway, she's on a different plane to them – or whatever Kev has planned, so you lot can have fun mounting a search and rescue operation." She grabbed her tray and swung round so fast the glass of water failed to combat the centrifugal forces urging it to spin and topple to the floor where it bounced, then smashed.

"Leave it, Jen. I'll sort it. Go watch your match." As he spoke, Ben grabbed another glass, filled it from the chiller and strode over with it. "I mean it. Go."

Her face wobbled as he set the glass on her tray. "Cheers." Anchoring it firmly, she left, just as Georgie headed in.

"Careful. Clean up on aisle two." Ben blocked her path as she wore no shoes.

She sidestepped. "Should I ask what happened?"

"Better not." He winked. "But we might not be Jen's favourite people right now."

"Tell me something I don't know. I probably should've warned you how she gets about Wimbledon."

"Can't think why we wouldn't have spotted–" Kev slapped his forehead. "Duh! It's been cancelled for the last two years because of the pandemic."

"It wasn't actually cancelled last year but she couldn't get tickets, so it was a bit of a non-event."

"I remember now. She spent a week in bed in July with summer flu." Isaac winked. "Or was it?"

"Whatever, she said we should carry on *Cursed Castle* without her. Are you up for that?" Kev put his arm round Georgie's shoulder. "Pretty please?"

She slid him a glance. "If you get on the floor and beg like a dog, I *might* consider it."

"Really?" He panted like a dog. "Should I lick your shoes?" More panting, with his hands bent in front of his chest like paws.

She pushed him away. "Forget it. I'll agree, on condition every session doesn't revert to me tapping into ghosts. Either you figure a way to do them as NPCs or one of the others can develop psychic abilities for a session."

"Your demands are high, fair lady, but I'm the man for the job." Another bow ending in an OTT flourish. "Woof woof." His yappy bark had her giggling.

After they'd all eaten, Ben found himself on the clearing up rota with Georgie, giving him a chance to chat. "Have you noticed something going on with Jen?"

"Were you not there? The whole 'tennis-fan-bot' thing."

"I meant apart from that. Can't think exactly when, but after years of on-the-edge-of-flirting banter, she's reverted to the reserve she distanced herself with at the start. All professional and aloof. I miss flirty-Jen." He pouted.

She nodded vigorously. "You too, huh?"

"Cool. I tried to think of something I'd done to offend her, but couldn't think of anything."

"Same. I couldn't decide if I was imagining it at first, but there's more than a hint of cold-shouldering going on. I don't understand it."

His eyebrow rose. "Thought you were thick as thieves."

"I would have agreed until the last few weeks; she's been like a true soul sister ever since we met."

Ben glanced around. "Back to the cloak and dagger stuff. I'd hate for her to walk in on us talking about her."

Georgie scoffed. "No chance of that, at least not for an hour. Djokovic's playing. Nuff said."

He glanced at her. "Don't shoot the messenger, but last time Kev mentioned about how she's often holed up with Isaac you got quite upset."

"I just hate that stupid song he sings. Brings back horrible memories from school." She shuddered.

"I'm sorry about that. I know Kev, and you have to believe his heart's in the right place. In his head he's cupid, matchmaking for his housemates."

She scoffed. "Nothing could be further from the truth." A beat. "You don't think … nah, never in a million years."

"What?" His eyes widened. "That they're …? No. Definitely not. She wouldn't – would she? You know her better than me, do you think she would?"

A snort. "As if. You watch them together outside of the campaign and tell me if that's real."

They both shook their heads simultaneously, and got on with the clearing.

~*~

Jen had mixed feelings about the kitchen incident, but the bust up meant they wouldn't disturb her so, on balance, it was a win. She didn't feel too badly about letting Kev know how much his neglect of her character sucked in the first few session. Until she spotted his hurt expression as she flounced out. Not a lot she could do about that now. With the change of direction, she was actually enjoying it, and really didn't want them to play too much without her, but it wasn't fair to ask them to wait. Of course, Ben had to be a perfect gentleman about her clumsiness, which ramped up the guilt even more. It meant when she asked for Thursday off in addition to the six days she'd booked, he agreed, no questions asked.

But the best-laid plans and all that – Isaac had booked the day off too and when she finally made it to the kitchen at nine thirty after a luxurious lie in, he was there with a freshly brewed pot of coffee, offering her a cup.

"Sit down, I have some croissants in the air-fryer – should be ready any minute."

"That's very kind, but I was just going to have fruit and yogurt, ta."

"One little croissant can't hurt. The sell by is today so it's that or the bin." His insouciance belied the fact he knew she'd been totally infected with Georgie's abhorrence of waste and would never let that happen.

But she let it go – a day off should always mean treats in her book. And they smelt wonderful – as did the pain-au-chocolat. But not as good as they tasted, dipped in the coffee and melting on her tongue.

After the barest minimum of small talk, he got to the real reason for his generosity. "How's it going with the inventory?"

"Sorry. I'm afraid it went to the bottom of the pile during the run up to the release."

"Understandably." Cradling his cup, he slid her a glance. "Remember a couple of weeks ago when I said about Georgie being up there doing it?"

She shook her head, collecting the empty mugs and swilling them ready for the dishwasher.

"I'm not complaining, believe me. Although I could, by rights, because after all that time, she'd hardly done anything."

"It's a long process. First you have to take a photo–"

"I know the process, I designed it."

"–and half the time, you can't even tell from that because you can only see the sleeve and can't tell if it's a coat or a dress–" She returned for the plates.

"She was doing the toys and games."

"That's just as bad because you can't read some of the writing on the boxes so you're up and down every couple of minutes, and–"

"But she wasn't. She was sitting down the whole time."

"Stop interrupting, I've told you, it's so rude."

He gestured at her to continue.

"I was going to say she's wasting her time trying to do it on her own. It's much easier with two people, one to shout it out and the other to type it in." She shut the dishwasher and leant against it.

His raised eyebrow ascertained she was finished before making it clear he had his own agenda. "Like I said before, I was worried – she was in there for so long each time and her vitals have shot up."

She frowned. "Hang on, how do you know how long she was in there?"

"As I said, I was concerned, so I checked the logs."

"Wait – the computer keeps a log of every time the door opens and closes?" She shrugged. "Of course it does."

"Among other things." He glanced away. "The point–"

"No. There's more to this. How come you know she was sitting down – is there a camera in there?" Her eyes flared as his gaze sought the wall. "To spy on people? That's despicable."

"It's a security measure and safety feature – if someone did fall asleep, it would trigger an alarm and I could check the feed on my laptop …" He spotted her face. "What?"

She reined in her outrage. "You've been spying on people for months."

"What? No. Why would I?"

"Why indeed? It's creepy."

"When I said I hadn't been spying on them, I meant I don't normally take much notice. But when that stuff went missing …" He broke off at her frown.

"What stuff?"

"I told you about it at the time, but you virtually bit my head off so I forgot about it for a while."

"Nope, can't remember – wait, is this about some dress-up clothes? They probably got returned to the wrong rack."

"I want to believe you, I do. But the evidence says otherwise. I'll show you."

Following him out, she checked her phone – she had plenty of time before play started at 11am, and the match on number one court wouldn't start till 1pm.

Her initial thought to humour him seemed vindicated when all he had to show her was grainy, black and white footage of them entering with all three garments. "But the blue skirt you borrowed is nowhere in the 50s rack."

"Did you check the 70s rack?"

"I couldn't see it in there."

"That's because you were looking with guy eyes. They only see what the brain allows them to." Opening the 70s cover she quickly ascertained the bright blue skirt was nowhere amid the browns, oranges and purples. But it captured her attention the instant she opened the 60s rack.

"See. All you had to do was think logically." Returning the outfit to the 50s rack, she spotted her blue swing coat and matching handbag. "How the heck did these get here?"

"Are they not part of the collection?"

"No. I got them from Vinted."

"Oh dear. But you can see why someone might have thought they belonged in here. They probably got scooped up accidentally. You should reclaim them."

"I certainly will." Putting them on the desk, she frowned, trying to remember when she'd last seen them in her wardrobe. *It was just a few days ago, wasn't it?*

"Now you see why the inventory is so important. I agonised over showing you this, but watch."

More crude footage, showing Georgie opening the game and handing the dice to Ben.

She frowned. "It'll be the same thing, they'll have put them back in the wrong box. Easily fixed. Which rack did she get it from?"

"The sixties. I think it was called Time Doctor or something. But before you check, the most urgent thing is the missing money." He handed over the 70s wallet. "This had over a hundred pounds in it. I checked and some of the collectors' items will fetch a couple of grand each."

She cleared space on the desk and carefully took out the notes, separating them into like value.

"While you do that, I'll nip to the loo. Back in a tick." He scuttled off, jiggling as the door took its time opening.

She counted three times, reaching the same total – £83 in notes and £2.66 in coins. When he didn't return after several hundred ticks, she retrieved the Time Doctors game and opened it on the desk. *What the what?* Two normal-ish six-sided dice. Picking them up, she examined the curious font, spotting numbers five to nine and something similar to the old-fashioned carriage return, line feed symbol still depicted on the return key of some keyboards.

The computer's three minute warning startled her and she nearly dropped one of the dice, but caught it. That was strange – *what happened to the ten minute one it normally gave?* Deciding to hang onto the dice to show Isaac how wrong he was, she grabbed her coat & bag, but the door refused to open when she typed in the code.

Refusing to panic, she returned to the computer. Isaac had discovered an emergency override sequence, and she typed it in, pressing enter.

"Emergency override activated. The door will open in … two … minutes."

Still no need to panic. From what she could remember, it would take several minutes for the air to be evacuated before the cleaning cycle began. It made sense to wear her coat to protect her clothes, but stress made her clumsy and, as she fumbled for the sleeve, she dropped the dice.

"Bugger." As she searched for them, a bright light filled the room, along with a vaguely familiar noise. Assuming this could be part of the detox, she hid under the desk.

Ch 7 – A Mad Cow and a Lady-killer

Cursed Castle

The professor chased after the others as fast as his impediment would allow, but he was not impressed when the Jester shouted at him. "Come on, slow coach, we need to get this door shut."

He was even less happy when the guy shoved him so hard he sprawled onto the floor. "There's no need to be quite so violent," he hissed.

"The prof's got the right idea. Down on the floor, torches off and keep quiet."

Rosalina dropped down without a sound, but Kurt dumped the heavy sports bag with a clatter, grumbling as he thumped down next to it and switched off his torch. "I will be expecting compensation for any equipment damaged by this."

Shaking his head, the professor voiced all their concerns. "What the hell was that thing?"

"What part of keep quiet do you not understand?" The jester's tone was the darkest yet.

The narrator described the scene with an unwarranted amount of repressed humour.

The ghost hunters huddled on the floor in the pitch black, hearing ominous sounds as the creature galloped around to the door they'd just entered, where it stopped with a bloodcurdling howl. Next, they heard loud sniffing and snorting as it pawed at the ground. They watched in trepidation as a humongous shadow stalked around the conservatory, much of which consisted of large glass windows misted up with the heat and humidity required to house the exotic plants. Finally, the shadow grew smaller as the creature backed off.

Grenville's immediate concern was for the women in the party. "Ladies, are you okay?"

Before they could answer, the entire structure trembled with an enormous crash. The narrator explained:

The beast had only retired a few paces and then rushed at the building head on. Luckily, it met with a sturdy door set into a solid brick wall. Several loud cracks indicated the surrender of glass panes to the forces involved, however, they remained intact. The thump of hooves and stumbling shadow spoke of the angry animal's disorientation before it finally lumbered off.

The narrator addressed Grenville. "If you really want me to answer your question about the nature of the beast, you'll have to roll at least an eight. But it's not your go."

Rosalina spoke up. "I am more than happy for the professor to go before me, because I can feel something coming through."

"As you wish." He rolled the dice on the professor's behalf, gaining eleven. "For that, I can tell you the beast, known as the Dun cow, stands as big as a double-decker bus. It came originally from Shropshire, but terrorised the people of Warwickshire for several weeks, destroying villages and devouring everything it met."

"But the important thing is, has it gone?" Kurt badgered. "Is it safe to leave?"

The narrator's tone held the same dark humour. "I'm sorry, but you will have to wait your turn."

"But that's not fair. You let *him* break the rules."

Grenville hid a secret smile. "Can you tell me any more about it?"

"The once-gentle creature could supply milk to all who needed it. But one day a witch tried to milk her into a sieve, which made the creature so angry she broke free, and has been wreaking terror ever since."

Kurt sniggered. "What is it with witches and sieves? Sorry, that was a different campa– I mean adventure involving a Scottish king."

The narrator didn't encourage him. "So now it's Evadne's go." Again with the dark, sardonic tone.

"Eva?" Kurt switched his torch on, flashing it around frantically. "Mein Gott! Where is she?"

"I can't believe you've only just noticed her missing." The jester sneered. "Fine friends you are."

"But it was pitch black and she was ahead of us …" He broke off, his anxiety evident.

The professor fumbled for his torch, playing the beam into various nooks and crannies. "She must be hiding."

"Because that sounds like the intrepid ghost hunter we all know and love." Rosalina's wry tone withered.

"I suggest you kill the lights and lower your voices unless you wish to attract the beast's attention." At the jester's words, Kurt shielded the beam.

"It's still out there?" Grenville scrambled to his feet. "We must find her – she's in danger."

"Now he cares. Did it not occur to any of you to check

everyone was safe?" More disdain. "Sit down, professor. If you barge out there on a hero's mission you will not survive. Use your most prominent muscle – your brain. And for goodness' sake dim that torch."

"Who's there?" Rosalina's voice took a pot-shot at doing 'old, wizened crone.'

The others immediately looked to the professor, so he took charge. "Peter Grenville, my lady. Do you need help?"

"Not from the likes o' you I don't. You'll be kin o' that Baron chap who thinks 'ee can lord it over us poor wretches because the king granted 'im the rights. Well 'ee don't 'ave the right o' me, that's for sure."

"I assure you, my lady–"

"Stop callin' me that. I ain't no lady, and neither's she, actin' the trollop an' spreadin' her legs for anyone as asks."

"Who is this – er, lively woman."

"Woman? Wanton more like. It's no wonder the 'orses get spooked with all the goings on." Her tone softened. "About your friend. I've bin sworn not to breathe a word, but if you want to find her, I can give you a riddle in return for a gold ring."

"Oohhh, I have one in my wallet." Kurt reached into his pocket for the wallet but it had disappeared.

"You reckon this is gold?" The jester held up what was obviously a curtain ring, and Kurt snatched it off him.

"It's a gold-coloured ring." He handed it to Grenville, who held it in the palm of his hand, snapping his fingers around it as she made a grab.

"Riddle first."

"You're not as green as you're cabbage-looking." She

cackled, then assumed a posh voice as she recited.

"My first is a secret never to be told,

My second is not steady like days of old.

My third sits next to a double letter,

And the whole will surprise – you thought you knew better."

Kurt had the foresight to have his notebook ready scribbling furiously. "What was the third line again?"

"That's for me to know and you to find out." She grabbed the ring with another cackle, and then exited sharply, leaving Rosalina gasping for breath.

Grenville offered her a water bottle as he gestured at Kurt. "Third is next to a double letter. Write it down."

"There was something about sitting."

"Sits next to a double letter. And the whole will surprise."

"You thought you knew better. Ja, I got that, it was only the third I stumbled with." He read the whole thing out again, scribbling. "The double letter must be M or W, so that gives us l, n, v or x."

"Not necessarily. You could argue that B is a double letter if you wrote it as a capital."

Kurt did so. "Ah yes. Double D." Ignoring the jester's snigger, he continued. "Reflected in a horizontal line instead of vertical like the others."

"By the same token, an X is double V."

"True." More scribbling. And at a push, a capital E is double C if you wrote it as a calculator would."

"A bit tenuous, but it gives us more choices, making the whole thing harder. Terrific." Grenville tutted.

"So a, c, d, f, l, n, v, w, x and y for the third."

The narrator stepped in. "May I suggest you're unlikely to solve this immediately, but in the meantime, you have been given a third clue pointing to an obvious place."

Rosalina stood, grabbing her bags. "Come on then, what are you waiting for?"

"Where are we going?"

"The stable, of course. Weren't you listening?" She strode off, the jester capering in front to open the door.

"What?" Kurt frowned. "How does she know that?"

"It was all there about the horses being spooked. Maybe turn your hearing aid up." He nudged him.

"Yes. *I* heard the crone say that, but how could Rosalina? If you remember, she said she had no memory of what Daisy said. She claimed not even to know it was a woman."

Grenville frowned as he collected the gear, then shrugged. "Could be it's practice improving her skills."

Kurt picked up his bag, shaking his head. "That's not right. Evadne's used her many times before – there's something strange going on." But he was talking to an empty room, and hustled after them.

As he caught up, the sound of galloping hooves filled them with dread, but it was a medieval knight, who pulled up aside them and raised the visor on his helmet.

"I must warn you, there is a monstrous beast abroad. I caution you to make your way to the nearest building as fast as possible. If you continue on for a few dozen yards, you will come to a fork, and the left path will take you to some stables, they are much closer than the castle."

"Thank you, Sir …?" Grenville raised expectant brows.

"Guy Gorian, known to some as Guy of Warwick. Hasten, for I hear its wail."

They cringed at the approaching bellow and, dropping his visor, he readied his lance and galloped at full tilt in the direction of the noise. Seconds later, they heard the sounds of conflict and the monster's scream of pain.

Rosalina scoffed. "How convenient for a hero to appear when we need one. And to reinforce our destination."

"If that's not the cherry on top." The jester winked. "And as good a place as any to search for trampled corpses. The stables it is."

She caught his arm, her tone fierce. "Eva isn't dead. I'd know if she were. She's in trouble, but I can't tell exactly what. I think someone has kidnapped her, and it's our job to solve the clues to find where they've hidden her."

The narrator called for a comfort break before shooting off downstairs. When they returned with the drink of their choice, he led them straight into the scene.

The jester led them into the half-brick, half-timber structure, where the dank, pungent smell assaulted their nostrils. Unaffected, Rosalina did a slow circuit around the main tack room while Kurt looked for suitable places to set up his equipment.

He stood in front of the girl, blocking her path. "Do you sense anything in here, or should we check each stall?"

"I can't imagine the horses will take too kindly to that. Maybe you could take a baseline reading in here to begin with." She glanced up at the hayloft. "I suspect if it could talk, that would have a few tales to tell."

Grenville spotted the ladder. "I suspect you're right." He began to climb, but had barely got halfway when an angry shout stopped him.

"Oy. What the fuck d'ya think you're doing?"

"Inspecting the hayloft, my good man." He piled on the accent. "And you are?"

"The guy telling you to get the fuck out of here." He spied Rosalina and his whole demeanour changed. "Sorry, sweetheart, didn't see you there. Pardon my French."

She waved it away with a smile designed to disarm. "I must apologise. We were led to believe it would be perfectly fine for us to continue our investigation in here."

"And who said it would be 'perfectly fine'? That pric— sorry, plank on the turnstiles?"

"Actually, it was …" She scanned the room for the jester, but he was nowhere to be seen. "Do you know, I never knew his name because Evadne sorted it all out. You haven't seen her have you? A tall blonde."

"Who?"

"Evadne Whyte, from the TV. You know, *Britain's Got Ghosts.*"

"Is this a wind up? Some sort of reality show? Are those four *Impractical Jokers* lunatics gonna jump out and hand me my arse on live TV? I can see the cameras – surely that's not how it works."

"What are you not understanding?" Kurt's intimidation attempt didn't work because the guy towered over him but, give him his due, the German didn't flinch. "We have permission to film in here, and we believe there is a ghost, most likely in the hayloft."

"Why didn't you say? Sure, there's a story about a stable lad back in the sixteen hundreds – I've done some digging and I believe we might be related."

"Really? Would you tell your tale for the camera?"

A shrug. "I guess. Where's this Eva chick? Did you say she was blonde?"

Kurt peered at Rosalina's outfit. "You'll have to ask the questions – we can always cut you out later."

"Charming." Greville continued to climb the ladder, but the newcomer shot over.

"Oy, Professor Bumble. I said, no-one's allowed up there. Get back here or I'll throw you off." He glared as Grenville climbed down, gesturing with two fingers pointing to his eyes, then at the professor.

"I take it that means you'll be watching me. Be my guest." He strode over to retrieve the meter he'd used. "I'll take the baselines, then?"

Kurt nodded, getting the light readings for the interview.

Rosalina smiled at the lad. "So, Mr …?"

"Tom Blackshaw. And what's your name, pretty lady?"

"You don't need to know. Just answer her questions without using her name."

"Alright, Herr Hitler, keep your hair on."

"My hair is perfectly well secured, thank you."

Having participated in several shows, Rosalina was more than capable of asking the right questions to unlock the tale about the amorous stable lad whose penchant for bedding local girls in the hayloft led to him observing a couple of conspirators from the November the fifth gunpowder plot to blow up parliament and kill King James.

"Isn't this a little far from London?" She frowned. "There were no express trains back then."

"True, and London was at least a day's ride away with several changes of horse. But this was much closer to home. Part of the plot was to snatch James' daughter Elizabeth from the abbot at Coombe Abbey and force her to become a puppet queen."

"So what happened to this medieval lady-killer?"

"He was blackmailed into spying for them or they would murder his family, and his sweetheart, Pol."

"They sound like a cut-throat bunch."

"You don't know the half of it. They forced him to steal horses and provisions for the journey."

"But the whole thing failed."

"Yes, and here's the kicker – after taking the horses to escape, they cut the throats of the pair of them up in that loft you're all so keen to explore."

"And why can't we?"

"Because it's a health and safety hazard. Floorboards are riddled with woodworm."

"One last thing. What was his name?"

"Dan Bloxham."

"Thank you very much, Tom."

He leapt up. "So when will this be on TV? I'll be famous. Won't have to buy a pint in Number One all year."

"Number One?" She tilted her head to the side.

"The Spoons in the market square. My local."

Kurt rustled some papers. "If I could just get you to sign this release form."

"What's that?"

"It gives us permission to show that on TV."

He stared at it, frowning.

"No signature, no free pints." Kurt pushed it at him.

Grabbing the pen, he scrawled in the three places marked with an X. "If you want any more tales, there's one about a spy during the siege as well."

"Another spy?"

"Yeah. Threw himself off the battlements, he did."

Grenville narrowed his eyes. "That sounds familiar. I remember something else about jumping off the battlements. I guess that's where we should go next."

Over dinner, Kev was keen to get feedback, and Isaac gave it to him straight.

"Not bad. Not the best by any means, but a lot better than I'd expected. Especially with only three of us."

"I reckon that Tom chappy was great fun. Totally irreverent, but it worked well." Georgie grinned.

Ben chuckled. "They do say write about what you know – he was basically a Kev clone."

"What about the riddle?"

"Don't say anything." Isaac virtually shouted. "I want to solve it without helpful clues. Preferably within the game."

"Which means you'll be up all night trying to figure it." Ben winked at Kev. "Good game, good game. Jen'll be sorry she missed it. Wonder what she's doing now?"

Ch 8 – Blast from the Past

June

Jen woke up with a thumping in her head at least equal to the worst migraine she'd ever suffered. She teased her eyes open the tiniest slit, and the luminous green attacking her optic nerve said she was outside somewhere. Snapping her eyelids to shut out the bright heat, she interrogated her other senses for further clues. Her body prickled with uncomfortable warmth and exploring fingers detected a coat, which she shrugged off, allowing the breeze access to her skin, which immediately cooled.

More exploration revealed she was sitting on wooden slats, and the metal arm-rest suggested an old-fashioned park bench. Shading her eyes, she risked a quick peek to confirm this. So, a bench in the middle of a park. How long had she been sitting there in her coat? Obviously not long enough for anyone to show any concern, but she reckoned most people would hurry past, no doubt writing her off as drunk or stoned in the judgy way people had. She couldn't imagine it happening in her gran's time – there would be at least half-a-dozen concerned passers-by enquiring after her health. *Why would she think of her gran?*

A shadow blocked some heat. "Are you all right, my dear? You look a little pale."

Blinking her eyes open, the figure in front of her could have been her gran – right down to the tweed skirt, sensible brown shoes and ubiquitous grey cardi – no matter how warm it got. All topped with a red felt hat with pink bow.

"I – it's a headache, nothing to worry about." She tried a

smile, but even that hurt.

She'd seen all the movies, and knew she'd eventually have to ask questions about where she was, but with the scorching sun blocked, her peripheral vision was rapidly gathering and collating information filling in blanks which suggested familiarity with the place.

"I'm guessing you're here for the tennis. It doesn't start for a wee while, how would you like a nice cup of tea and a slice of cake to put some colour back in your cheeks?"

Her mouth felt positively Saharan, and food always grounded a migraine. "That sounds wonderful, thank you. I'm sure there'll be a Costa around here somewhere."

"Acosta? Never heard of it. But I live just across from the park, and was just on my way back for elevenses. Do you feel strong enough to stand?"

"Of course, thank you." She folded the coat over her arm and picked up the bag lying beneath it. Gritting her teeth, she rose slowly, determined not to show any weakness which would result in undue concern.

"Atta-girl. We'll walk slowly to let your head settle – it's only a few minutes away. Where are my manners? I'm Betty Cartwright. Pleased to meet you."

"Jen Paulson." She shook the outstretched hand. "Thank you for coming to my rescue."

When she got to the path, all the puzzle pieces clicked into place. This was the massive park in Wimbledon opposite the All England Lawn Tennis & Croquet Club. *Where she was supposed to be tomorrow.* Always assuming it was still June the thirtieth. She could ask, but that would alert the woman to a potential memory loss, then she'd be insisting on a trip to A&E – she certainly looked the type. Well, that explained her thinking of her gran – she'd been brought up in one of the nearby houses.

Something niggled – the park didn't look quite right, but she couldn't figure out why. When they walked out onto the street, it got more obvious. While the tournament was on, the road was normally packed with the cars of people who refused to pay exorbitant parking fees and didn't want to use the park and ride. But apart from a couple of vintage cars parked in the driveways, there wasn't a car in sight.

For as long as she could remember the residents and visitors had battled over parking – maybe the penalties had become more than made it worth the risk. She couldn't spot any obvious restrictions, but the government was well into stealth taxes with all the emission zones and stuff. It was probably all done by virtually invisible cameras, and the DVLA computers would issue the fines automatically, rubbing their metaphorical hands with undue glee. Big brother crap was everywhere these days, spying and punishing, all down to people like herself writing software that ultimately stuck it to the man in the street.

"Nearly there."

Returning her smile, Jen was suddenly reminded of Bathilda Bagshot – the creepy woman in Godric's Hollow who turned into Voldemort's pet snake, Nagini. Even more so when the house whose drive she entered had a similar façade. But that was just a story, and this was definitely NOT a Harry Potter movie. The landscaped front garden positively rioted with colour and rich summer scents, and Jen thought how most people would have ditched the display in favour of an extra couple of parking places.

Going through the front door was like walking into a set on Foyle's War, or any Second World War movie. Old, worn-but-sturdy furniture hosted lovingly crocheted doilies, and lacy antimacassars protected every seat back and arm rest. Exactly like in her gran's house. But instead of modernising the walls with textured paint or vinyl wallpaper, it had the thick, almost-fabric wallpaper she'd torn off every wall in her mum's house. Except this was in the original, bright colours instead of darkened to nicotine brown by years of people smoking in the house, added to decades of wallpaper paste from the layers of paper pasted over the top. The print was similar to that in her room.

Removing her hat, Betty regarded her curiously. "Do you like it? I didn't think young things like you would be interested in anything so mundane as wallpaper patterns."

She blushed. "I love these vintage styles, they look almost hand-painted."

"Vintage? This is the latest design from Debenhams."

"It looks as though you only put it up last week. The colours are so vibrant."

"Why thank you. Come through and I'll put the kettle on." She led her into a kitchen worthy of a retro-design article in an interior design magazine and filled the kettle, setting it on the gas ring to boil, and spooning actual loose-leaf tea into a teapot. *Each to his – or her – own.*

Jen gazed past the bulky refrigerator and authentic-looking oven with eye-level grill, wondering where all the normal counter-top-cluttering devices were. No microwave, bread-maker or espresso machine – apart from the toaster and percolator, the only other appliance was a sturdy electric mixer. Instead of a dishwasher or washer/dryer next to the sink unit, she spotted a strange contraption which looked like her gran's old top-loading washing machine, but with a strange contraption on the top. Peering closer, she tried to figure out what it was.

Having, laid out the cups and plates, Betty joined her. "It's a beaut, isn't it? That wringer will take all the work out of doing it by hand. Especially the bed sheets."

Blimey – that was taking the whole green thing a bit far. But she expected praise. "I've never seen anything like it."

She beamed. "I'm so lucky John's got a good job and can afford to lavish me with all the mod cons. But you need them, running a guest house."

"I know. My family ran one a down the street–"

"I'll bet they're as full as I am – it's always the same in June/July, we're so convenient for the tournament. What's the name? I probably know them."

Jen was saved the need to answer by the kettle whistling its completion, and she took the three tier cake stand over to the table as Betty brought over the tray with the tea things, including a milk jug.

"Goodness me. I feel like royalty. Or at least as though I'm in one of those posh hotels that do afternoon tea."

"Bless you, pet. This is just the everyday stuff, I'm afraid, because Monday's laundry day." She stirred the pot and then poured the tea through a strainer – again, a lot less wasteful, but so much hassle.

Sharing a delightful – and very English – ritual with this sweet, undemanding woman made Jen realise there were still people in the world who valued life's simple pleasures. A real throwback, as her gran would say. Okay, some of her attitudes harked back several decades, but Jen reckoned it was a generation thing. When *she* hit her forties – or even fifties – Jen couldn't see herself being satisfied with a lifestyle which didn't require her to use her brain for anything more demanding than working out a shopping list to cater breakfast for seven houseguests.

Betty chatted about the awful rain storms, the rising price of everything and an explosion which sank a submarine in Dorset killing thirteen crew members.

"Oh dear, I hadn't heard."

"It was all over the news at the time, but my husband served in the Navy, so we're keeping up with the latest." She tapped the newspaper article. "They've raised the wreck and suspect it might have been a faulty torpedo." She shivered. "Sorry, love. I didn't mean to get so morbid. It's all doom and gloom at the moment, what with the rail strike and the state of emergency and everything."

Jen nodded, having just taken a bite of a melt-in-your-mouth rock cake, relishing the heavenly taste.

"That'll be the cinnamon. It's good to see a youngster enjoying her food. So many today are on silly diets, wanting to look like film stars." She sipped her tea. "Yes, it was a right shame they had to cancel the trooping of colour because of the rail strike – that poor prime minister has had so much on his plate since he came into power."

"You're not wrong there." *But the trooping of the colour wasn't cancelled – Georgie had watched it all.*

"He's obviously doing something right to win the

general election – he nearly doubled the majority that Churchill got. But my John thinks he was right to retire; they said it was due to ill-health, but 80's far too old to be running the country."

Jen frowned. *Why would she be talking about Churchill?* That was decades ago, after the war.

"John reckons Eden's doing the best he can, but it's like the whole country's against him at the moment."

Prime Minister Eden? *What the what?* Jen's knowledge of political history was pretty dire, but she was sure he was back in the fifties. Back when people boiled water on the stove and used wringers on their sheets. And no freezers or dishwashers. Those weren't vintage collectors' cars she'd seen, they were brand new. *Computer says no.*

"Are you all right, love? You've gone white as a sheet."

"I'm fine, thank you. I've taken up enough of your valuable time." She glanced at the clock. "I should make my way to the club, the queues should have gone down."

Getting up slowly, she avoided the blood rush.

"I imagine you'll want to use the little girl's room before you go. It's just to the left of the front door."

Do what? So many euphemisms for toilet, but she'd not heard anyone use this one except her great gran.

"Thank you, I'd appreciate that." The moment alone gave her time to rationalise. One of the lads at work had taken a summer job in a care home and had a stack of stories of how some dementia patients could only cope by being surrounded by artefacts from the time they felt most at home. So their rooms were like stepping back into a different decade. *And who was she to judge?* All their

95

bedrooms were monuments to a bygone age.

Feeling a lot happier, she washed her hands with the pungent lifebuoy soap and went out with renewed energy.

"Oh that's better. I was going to suggest I might accompany you to make sure you made it intact."

"That's very sweet, but you've done so much. Thank you again for your kindness, you're my guardian angel."

A scoff. "Be off with you. Anyone would have done the same. And it's done me the power of good to have a nice young lass to brighten my day. If you find yourself nearby at this time, you must pop in. I'm here every day taking a little break, and I'm usually on my own."

"I'd love to." Despite everything, she really meant it.

Betty accompanied her to the front door, standing on the top step and waving to her until a tree obscured her view.

Jen scoured her surroundings for more clues, noting how clean and beautifully maintained everything was, and how few driveways had room to park a car, let alone a garage. But the most striking thing had to be the lack of traffic on the road – this was normally a busy thoroughfare. Of course – it'll be a deliberate closure – either for the tournament, or ubiquitous roadworks.

She rang the doorbell and stepped back, recalling a recent conversation about where her gran lived, but couldn't think who it was with. The girl who opened the door was the spitting image of her gran – not as she remembered her, but the seventeen-year-old in the photo, holding the Wimbledon junior championship trophy.

Fireworks went off in Jen's brain and she slumped to the floor.

Ch 9 – A Deadly Secret

Cursed Castle

The narrator summarised the previous session.

If you remember, at the end of our last session, our intrepid adventurers lost one of their party, the gorgeous Evadne. So now they have a second quest – to find the courageous ghost hunter and bring her back to the team. You'll notice I didn't say rescue her, because if ever a girl didn't need a knight in shining armour, it's her. Although there is one available if either of you ladies need it. And let me be clear – I'm not talking about the lovely Rosalina.

Rosalina chuckled. "Thanks for that vote of confidence, but in my head he *was* rather yummy."

The professor scowled. "If you two will stop flirting, we need to ensure we're not taking anything for granted. I think we should engage the staff in a thorough search of the Castle and grounds." He held up his hand as Rosalina prepared to argue. "I know you're confident she's alive, but she may be lying somewhere, bound and gagged."

Kurt bristled. "I know her better than any of you and I wouldn't discard the possibility she has already escaped and is merely lying low somewhere. She may not have heard Sir Guy defeating the Dun Cow."

"True." Grenville's brows beetled. "We need to think as she would. Where would she go?"

"I won't be happy until I've checked out that hayloft. There's so many bad vibes up there it has to be top of the list after Tom took such pains to keep us away."

The professor stroked his chin. "That could be tricky – we need to find a way to distract him. Normally, I'd suggest Evadne and, in her absence, Rosalina is the obvious choice, but she needs to be inside."

Kurt sniffed. "I'll get him to take some stills around the castle and talk about this spy in the battlements."

"Sounds like a plan." Grenville glanced at his watch. "We have twenty minutes before meeting the jester, this may be our only opportunity to do this without him."

"I take it you don't trust him either?" Kurt frowned.

A scoff. "We'll stay out here – make sure you keep him away for at least fifteen minutes to give us time."

Kurt frowned. "What are you expecting to find?"

Rosalina shivered. "I don't know, but it's definitely something very dark."

"Good luck."

"You, too."

Hiding behind some pungent bushes, they watched as he strode into the block and, scant minutes later, saw him emerge, emf-detector in hand.

Tom looked sceptical as he hurried to catch him up. "You reckon that thing is picking up the trail of blood? How is that possible when it's centuries old?"

Kurt scoffed. "You wouldn't understand the science. But you saw how it went berserk near the hayloft."

"That was mental."

"Every dastardly act has a dark energy which imprints itself into the surroundings, and certain materials – such as wood, and particularly stone – retain those vibrations for centuries. People call it an ectoplasmic residue."

"Like on *Ghostbusters*. And that machine picks it up? What's the betting we'll find the bodies?"

"Slim, I'd say. The trail's heading for the gatehouse."

He hurried off, the eager lad in tow. After waiting till they were out of sight, the professor grabbed Rosalina's hand, guiding her into the stables. He tried the door, surprised to find it unlocked. "Strange. I'd have expected him to secure it."

"But you saw how engrossed he was with the machine and Kurt didn't give him time to dawdle."

Inside, a dim low-light designed not to disturb the horses created an eerie glow. Grenville hurried to the ladder, climbing up to the hayloft and helping her up the last few steps. "What should I do?"

She shrugged. "You could try recording it on your phone, but don't be surprised if it doesn't pick up much."

"I meant what should I do if something nasty tries to take you over – or attack you? Like the witch."

"The best way of breaking the connection is to shock me back to the present. A dowsing in cold water works."

"Excellent, I'll get my water bottle ready."

"I'm sorry, Dan. I didn't mean for it to happen." Her voice had changed, and she was no longer Rosalina, but a throwback to days of yore.

"Girls like you never do." The venom sent chills making Grenville shudder as he searched for the voice's owner.

"But it doesn't have to be the end for us. The wise woman can give me a potion to make it go away."

"No, Pol. If you really wanted that, you'd have done it by now, not left it until you're showing in the hope you can trap me into a loveless marriage."

"But Dan, you said you loved me."

"I'll say anything to have my wicked way." His ugly sneer grated. "You of all people should know that."

"I know you say that to the rest of them, but I thought–"

"That's where you went wrong. Girls like you start thinking, they get all manner of wrong ideas. Well, it's not going to happen. No bitch will ever snare Dan Bloxham."

"Of course. I'll get rid of it, Dan. It's not too late."

"It is for you." The shadow loomed closer, gaining substance, and Grenville saw the glint of a blade aiming for her throat.

"Nooooo!" He dashed forward, snatching her out of harm's way, feeling the snick of metal against his ear. They crashed to the ground and he glanced back to see the malevolent figure dissolve into blackness.

Rosalina had lost consciousness and, with a muttered apology for the lack of dignity, he slung her over his shoulder in a fireman's lift, allowing his free hand to cling onto the ladder as he carried her away from the dreadful place. Mindful of the time, he dribbled water into her mouth, wanting to revive without soaking her.

She jerked up, coughing, and he offered her the bottle. Taking a sip, she choked, banging on her chest before trying again. When she spoke, her voice cracked. "Wasn't expecting that. What a shitbag."

He chuckled. "Indeed. However it does bring into question Tom's motives – did he genuinely not know, or was he trying to cover up for his fellow stable lad?"

"I'd like to give him the benefit of the doubt – wait –

what's that on your ear?"

He felt the wetness and inspected the dark stain.

"You're bleeding."

He produced a large white handkerchief, pressing it to his ear. "Probably just a scratch."

A scoff. "Without wanting to conform to the trope, let me sort it." She took the hankie, dampening it from his water bottle and cleaned it, surprised at the amount of blood. Fetching a tissue from her bag, she tore off a scrap and squeezed it over the cut to slow the flow.

A distant noise had them jumping up and dashing out just as the jester and Kurt came into view. Grenville peered past, but could see no sign of the stable lad.

~*~

Never one to voluntarily put himself in even the slightest threat, Kurt surprised himself by volunteering to act as decoy, but it made sense as he'd have the best chance of duping Tom. So far, so good – the lad seemed too simple to have any knowledge of even vaguely technical equipment, let alone something with so many settings on the dial and a complex readout. He seemed happy to accept the beeping meant the presence of ectoplasm, as they hurried through the courtyard like dogs on the scent of a trail. There was no need to rush, but like any good director, he knew how much more dramatic a chase made things, and he dashed into the gatehouse where Tom took the lead.

Kurt wasn't very good at subterfuge, but he couldn't see any other strategy which might result in the return of his partner-in-crime, as she liked to style herself. He never understood the phrase, unless it referred to the occasions where their investigations resorted to borderline illegal activities in the pursuit of their ghostly goals. Or should that be ghouls? Suppressing a snigger as they climbed a second staircase, he realised her influence had impacted on his normally scrupulous integrity. But not in a bad way, merely a "loosening up," as she put it, of his natural obduracy. Also known as cold-hearted pig-headedness.

"Hey, Fritz. How come it's stopped beeping?" Tom indicated the instrument.

"I – er – the signal must be getting weaker."

"Maybe all the blood had dripped out of them." A ghoulish chuckle.

"Quite. Is it much further?"

"Just one floor. Quite the climb, isn't it?"

"I imagine much worse if you were carrying a couple of dead bodies."

"But there would have been enough of them to spread the load. Ah, here we are." He led the way to the top level with crenellations between the two towers. He took him to the edge, pointing down towards the river. "See those black and white houses on Mill Street? They were built many centuries ago and during the siege, the Cavaliers tried to use them as cover in one of their sorties."

Despite his severe dislike of heights, Kurt peered down, quickly stepping back as his vivid imagination had him watching himself pitching forward and tumbling arse-over-tip onto the barbican. "Your point being?"

He shrugged. "Simply that there's more to leaping off battlements than meets the eye." A wink. "Whatever you may hear, it's doesn't necessarily mean certain death."

"True. And what would be the point of throwing a body from here? It would just land on the building below or in the moat with every opportunity for discovery."

"Now you're getting it. So unless that thing of yours can actually detect anything more than fluctuations in the magnetic field which may or may not indicate something paranormal, you're not going to find much here without your pretty psychic's help."

"In that case, we should fetch her."

"That would be wise, yes. Means you'll have to climb all these stairs again, but I suspect that still won't make you as breathless as your professor mate." A meaningful nod.

On the way down, he gave a few hints about the siege and Kurt made a mental note of the names, intending to verify them – something about this so-called stable lad felt a bit off. Then he disappeared with a cheeky, "Places to go, people to be."

Kev suggested they knock it on the head for the night, saying he had a couple of adjustments to make, and Isaac stayed behind for a word while the other two went down to make a start on the meal.

~*~

After dinner, the unlikely pair went to play a session of Team Fortress, and Ben sat with Georgie, flicking through the channels and landing on Richard Curtis's excellent movie, *About Time*. It was around twenty minutes in, but they'd both seen it before, and it seemed an apt cover for the things on his mind. The premise was even more far-fetched than dice: the characters merely had to find a dark cupboard, clench their fists and think of where – and when

– they wanted to be.

"Disbelief well and truly suspended." Ben grinned.

"I know, right. But it's cleverly done – really makes you think about all the ramifications of altering the time line."

"Yeah. I've been thinking about Eric."

"Me too. We didn't discover what triggered his time travelling."

"But we do know it hadn't happened in 1977 – there was no sign of the time capsule in the attic back then."

"That's another thing. How come the materials used to build it are so space-aged? Surely that seamless white finish wasn't available last millennium."

"They certainly had fibreglass by then."

"Of course. But the way the entrance door and keypad both disappeared looked proper futuristic."

"Not with today's technology – consider what they did with those double decker buses at the pageant."

"Whatever." Georgie frowned. "The point I'm trying to make is stuff like that wouldn't have been available in the late nineties when he disappeared, so he must have come back at some point afterwards."

"Unless – no."

"What?"

"I suppose it's possible, but no way I'd have put him down as that skilled an actor. Especially after his attempts to play a half-wit ogre in Jen's *Tangled Warren*."

"Isaac? I'd agree he couldn't act his way out of a paper bag, but what's that got to do with the price of cheese?"

He snorted. "Any more clichés you'd like to mix in?"

She glared. "Stop stone-walling and tell me what you

think Isaac's done. Oh." Revelation hit. "You think Isaac did all the modern stuff. But he was as knocked out by the whole thing as any of us."

"Was he?" A pause. "Think back."

Her eyes narrowed. "First of all, if he'd been doing all that, the lock wouldn't have rusted closed, and there would have been far more footprints in the dust. You saw the effect when we went back to 1977."

"Yes, but we wouldn't have noticed any footprints amongst everything else to look at. And he could easily have done something to jam the lock."

"Then there was the whole, 'Wait, I should go first' when Jen finally got the door open. He could have been in there scattering dust over everything."

"On balance it's unlikely he'd even think of it."

"Let's not forget the crocodile tears whenever anyone mentioned Eric or especially Naomi."

"Classic distraction technique."

"And how he disappeared for a while before 'discovering' the time capsule."

"And pretending to get the code wrong the first time."

"Oh my God. You could attribute all his actions on the first visit being driven by him knowing all about it."

"Except all the stuff about the toys – he sounded quite authentic when he dissed the Tamagotchi."

"But he soon activated the computer – he must have known about the hermetic seal and the dust monitor."

"Unless that was just something he set up to keep us out while we did the attic up. He certainly has the skills."

"So if he knew it all, why hasn't he been travelling

through time like it was going out of fashion? He's at least as obsessed with it as Sheldon."

The discussion took a back seat as the movie drew them in. At the end, he spotted her wiping away a tear and scooched over to give her a hug. "What are you like?"

She pulled back. "I know. Stoopid movie. And kinda mental after going through it." A shudder. "But that whole scene in the haystack was a bit close to the knuckle."

"What haystack? I don't remember that bit."

"In Warwick Castle."

"You've got to hand it to Kev, he's really turned it around. But you weren't actually scared, were you."

"Not so much scared as – I dunno – moved? Touched? Whatever, I think it's gonna rob me of some sleep."

"Not if we give your mind something else to think about. I've been putting it off for a while, but you know when I didn't return to 1977 straight away?"

"I finally get to find out where you went." She clapped her hands.

"Kind of. Remember in Deathly Hallows after Voldemort kills Harry, there's a scene at King's Cross station, where he meets Dumbledore?"

Her eyes widened. "You saw Dumbledore?"

"No, but –"

"Voldemort killed you?"

"No." He chortled.

"You went to King's Cross station?" She deadpanned.

"No. Stop." He looked like he was in pain.

"So it was nothing like the deathly hallows, then."

A gulp of laughter burst out. "Stop, you're killing me."

"Which is more than Voldemort did." She grinned, watching as he fought to regain control.

"Brat." He glared. "There was no need for torment."

"On the contrary, that's exactly what you put me through, disappearing like that."

"I didn't mean to, I promise." He sobered. "But it felt–"

"Like you'd died and gone to heaven?"

"More like I was in some kind of limbo."

"Hence the whole King's Cross station thing."

"Exactly."

"Got there in the end. How long did it last? Your time in limbo, I mean."

"No idea. Felt like a couple of seconds."

"I didn't have a watch, but it felt more like ten minutes to me. Enough time for Eric and the other version of you to stash a couple of trestle tables."

"Sounds about right." He shook his head. "So. Many. Stairs. Those things get real heavy, real quick."

"Tell me about it." She nodded. "But when my version of you finally arrived, you were coughing and choking, whereas I was fine. Curious."

"And then we were both okay on the fourth jaunt."

"I wondered if that might be because we'd come home."

He shrugged. "One thing's for sure. If we do it again, we take essentials like water and painkillers."

"Travel-sickness pills. Maybe plasters – a first aid kit."

"We'll make a list and add to it every time we remember something. But definitely water."

His distraction tactic worked and, when she got to bed, she went out like a light and slept the sleep of the dead.

Ch 10 – Wonderful Wimbledon

June 1955

When she woke up this time, Jen was lying on something hard which quickly revealed itself as a floor covered in the same patterned lino in her gran's house, but several shades lighter than she remembered. She was curled on her side in the recovery position with a soft cushion under her head.

"Oh, thank goodness." Then, louder. "Mum, it's fine, she's awake." Despite being several decades younger, there was no mistaking her gran's voice.

Jen had a few moments to decide her play, and reasoned the best tactic would be to feign total disorientation and memory loss while she assessed her options. And, like the best schemes, it wasn't far from the truth. She cleared her throat, her voice croaking nicely. "Where am I?"

"Hello, Miss. Don't try to speak. You're in Wimbledon in London, and you've had a funny turn. My name's Vickie and my mum's Dora. She's having to rest because she's broken her leg, but she's quite worried about you."

Jen tried to raise herself, but the ghost of her recent migraine reared up, suggesting she not move too fast as she managed to prop herself up on an elbow.

"Take it easy. Here, have a sip of this." She held a small glass to Jen's lips, tilting it slightly. "It's only cooking brandy, but it's supposed to be good for shock."

The piquant liquor burnt as it trickled down her throat and, resisting the strong urge to cough, Jen relaxed, letting the warmth spread throughout her chest area.

"T-thank you." She waved away the offer of a second sip, and pushed herself into a sitting position, resting a beat to let her head equalise.

"Give it a moment – coach says your brain needs extra time to catch up after a fall." She giggled. "Sorry, I should explain. I play tennis, but I don't fall over often – at least, I haven't done for a while."

Jen narrowed her eyes – should she let on that she knew who she was? Maybe, but not yet, not until she'd figured a cover story.

"Oh dear – are you in pain?"

"No. I'm simply struggling to remember anything."

"That's not good. You may have banged your head when you fell." Her eyes darted down the hall. "We should call a doctor."

Oops. Better show rapid signs of recovery. She made a show of examining her head. "No sign of any lumps." A warm smile. "I had a headache a short while ago, it's probably the remains of that."

"Nothing a cuppa can't fix, eh? Let me help you up."

Nothing could have prepared Jen for the sensation of physical contact with her gran – her individual scent brought back many vivid memories and she had to force herself not to cling on in a totally inappropriate hug.

"You seem a little unsteady – lean on me while we get you into the parlour."

Jen's great gran was already in her seventies when Jen was born, so she only had vague memories of a white-haired old lady in a wheelchair. The woman she now met had the kind of no-nonsense energy of someone who'd taken an active part in a world war.

"Pleased to meet you." Her handshake was firm and energetic. "Sorry I can't get up, but the doc says I need to rest or I could do permanent damage." She gestured at the plaster cast enclosing her left leg from thigh to foot.

"And we must always do as doctors say, right?" Jen's eyes twinkled as she repeated her gran's cheeky mantra.

She scoffed. "I could certainly tell a tale or two. Vickie, love. Stick the kettle on, would you? And use the good china." Gesturing at the armchair next to hers, she instructed Jen to sit down, "Till I get a proper look at you."

Jen had to bite her tongue not to reveal she knew all about Dora's exploits as an ambulance driver and triage nurse, racing through London's bombed-out streets in the blitz. The stories were legendary among the family, and a photo of her wearing the medal presented by King George held pride of place on the mantelpiece next to the photo of Vickie holding the Wimbledon junior cup.

"What did you say your name was?" Her tone bordered on the stern side of neutral.

She blinked as though trying to remember. "Jen, I mean, Jennifer Paulson, but everyone calls me Jen."

"Jen it is, then. We don't stand on ceremony in this house. And where's your husband? I can't believe he's letting you wander around Wimbledon on your own."

"I'm not married, Mrs …?"

"Potts. Dora Potts."

Jen widened her eyes. "So your daughter must be Victoria Potts, the tennis champion. I thought she looked familiar." She held the sides of her face. "What you must think of me, invading your home."

But whatever she thought was lost as Vickie came in bearing a plate with a large Victoria sponge missing a couple of slices. "Mum's been showing me how to bake my namesake cake – it's nothing like as good as hers."

"Rubbish, you're simply fishing for complements. But you know I never give them." A grim chuckle, and then she addressed Jen. "Would you mind being mum?"

"Of course." Thankfully, she'd watched enough old movies to know this meant she should cut the cake, and she placed the knife at what she assumed would be a reasonable slice, but Dora huffed.

"No wonder you're as thin as a rake if that's your idea of a decent portion. You can double it for me, and Vickie's a growing girl. Yours should be even bigger – men like a girl with a bit of meat on her bones."

Vickie reappeared with a tray as Jen cut the third slice, and she was thankful when her teenage gran poured, not trusting herself to manage the tea-strainer without making a mess. Sitting back in her chair, she surveyed the monster wedge, filled with jam and buttercream, her instincts wondering how many miles to run it off. Then her mind reminded of the impossible situation and she focussed on information gathering. But her host had the same mission.

"Presumably you've come for the tennis, then? Do you have a ticket for today?"

Hedging her bets, she told the truth. "I had tickets for the second week." She scanned around. "My handbag."

"Don't worry, it's here." Dora passed it over with a frown. "I hope you don't mind, but we peeked inside to see if we could spot something with your name on it."

Jen's brain froze, knowing money looked completely different back in the fifties with huge notes and strange coins like threepenny bits and farthings. The game would be up if they'd looked in her purse. It would be indiscreet of her to open it – they may think she was accusing them of stealing. But it would be unnatural not to check. It wasn't even her purse, and she opened it to see unfamiliar notes. The frown and hostile tone said she'd made a huge blunder.

"Don't worry, we didn't touch your money."

"It's not that. I – I." She frowned, seeking something which wouldn't worsen her situation.

A sniff. "Well, I must confess, we were perplexed when we found this." She passed over a thin wallet, and Jen opened it to see a perfect facsimile of a driving licence dated from 11 March 1953 until 10 March 1956.

"But so far your story holds up. Although we were surprised about the Miss. It didn't seem right, a lovely girl like you still on the shelf." Finally, the ghost of a smile.

Jen sought the reassurance of conformity, copying the idioms. "I'm walking out with a chap, but he travels a lot."

"Of course he does. It seems since the war most chaps are struggling to find jobs. What did he do?"

Jen glanced away, trying to work out how old her supposed young man would have been a decade ago.

Dora slapped her hand to her mouth. "Oh, I understand. He was one of those smart codebreakers and you're not allowed to talk about it." Her eyes widened. "I'll bet you were, too – you have that manner. It explains the driving licence, and the address in West Bletchley."

Giving thanks for the gift, Jen assumed the expected demeanour. "I'm sorry, but I couldn't possibly affirm or deny your statement." She gave an exaggerated wink, hoping she'd never be expected to justify the claim, despite watching her fair share of Bletchley-based shows.

Vickie's hands went up to her cheeks and she sighed. "Oh my, this is so exciting – wait till I tell Laura. And Shirley will just die–"

"Absolutely not." Dora almost growled. "Loose lips sink ships, remember."

"Oohhh, Mu-um. The war finished ages ago."

Jen tried to look suitably supportive, but this was pushing her acting talents to the limit in her fragile state, and she surreptitiously checked the rest of the handbag to find it contained little apart from a plain white handkerchief, retro-looking lipstick and compact, a tiny tin of Vaseline and a long, thin box with a Maybelline logo. None of which belonged to her.

"Well you certainly seem genuine enough. If it's not too much of an imposition, I wonder if you might accompany Vickie to the afternoon session."

She cocked her head. "Is there a problem?"

"Apart from the obvious?" Dora gestured at her cast.

Jen's instincts wanted to question whether a seventeen-year-old needed a chaperone, but her silence was rewarded.

"Oohhh, Mu-um. I told you, I'm nearly eighteen. I do *NOT* need a chaperone."

"Her mother's face hardened. "You *know* why."

Vickie glanced down. "You'll think I'm imagining things, but I keep getting the feeling I'm being watched."

113

"I've told you, Vickie, it's not only you. I've had that weird prickling sensation too."

"A couple of times, I spotted a staring face. I couldn't put my finger on it, but there was something not quite right about it." She shrugged. "But as soon as I turned, he simply dissolved into the crowds."

Jen tightened her jaw. "That sounds spooky. Maybe you have a stalker."

"A poacher?" They both frowned.

"Not quite. Someone who stalks after famous people – like Marilyn Munroe."

"Oohhh, I can imagine after *Gentleman Prefer Blondes*. It was very racy."

"Don't be putting ideas in her head." Dora's finger scolded. "There's a huge difference between a young tennis player and an international film star."

"Of course there is. But surely the security staff wouldn't let anything happen to you."

"Exactly. I'll be fine."

"How about I just accompany you to the gate? After all, I'm going in the same direction."

"That would set all our minds at rest." Dora smiled.

Jen did a quick mental calculation, pleased to see her mental faculties returning. "You *are* the reigning girl's champion after all."

Vickie pouted. "True, which is why I need to be there, even though I'm out of women's singles."

More brain racking. "It was a German woman – somebody Schmitt?"

"Suzanne's actually French. What a disaster, going out

in straight sets in the first round."

Dora snorted. "It's no shame to lose to someone so experienced. She must be nearly thirty if she's a day."

"It was total humiliation. I couldn't even hold my serve in the second set. I might as well give up."

"Don't say that. You're the current girl's champion and you were runner up the year before. There's no shame losing to much more experienced women."

As Dora beamed her approval, Jen tapped into a rich store of information which suggested he'd recently mugged up for *Mastermind*, with Vickie Potts as her specialist subject. "And look how well you did against that American in your first go at the women's title. How many British girls can even say they've played at Wimbledon?"

"Plenty. Shirley and I were counting them up. Thirty nine of the ninety six who qualified were British. That's forty percent."

Jen couldn't be sure of the exact figures, but she was pretty sure there were less than ten in 2022. She needed to reassure. "But these are all women, you have years, yet."

She wouldn't be consoled. "I'm already older than Mo Connolly was when she won Wimbledon – with an injured shoulder. And she won the US Open at sixteen. But now she's had to retire. What a waste."

Dora shook her head. "I've given up trying to talk some reason into her. But maybe you can."

Jen smiled. "I'd be delighted."

"Where are you staying, my dear?"

More brain freeze. But once again, her guardian angel had her covered as the doorbell rang, and Dora asked her to accompany Vickie – "Just in case."

Thinking furiously about alternatives involving her luggage getting stolen, she stared as Vickie opened the door to nothing but a suitcase.

"That's strange, there's nobody there. What do you make of that?"

Jen squeezed past her, checking up and down the street, but it was deserted.

"Curiouser and curiouser. The label has this address, but the name's Jennifer Paulson. Oh, is that you?"

"Yes." She stared at the unfamiliar case.

"But why would you put our address on it?"

"Who is it, love?" Dora's anxiety had Vickie running back to the parlour, carrying the case, and Jen followed, wondering how exactly she could explain this.

"It's the strangest thing. Somebody dropped this off and then ran away."

"Who would do that? What did he look like?

"I didn't see anyone. The label says Jennifer Paulson, but she doesn't recognise it."

"Was it your young man?"

Jen shook her head. "I didn't see anyone either. I'm sorry. I'm just as confused as you are."

"Well, there's only one thing for it, we'll have to open it up. Sit down, my dear. You look a little wobbly."

As she complied, Vickie set the case on the floor, her tone matching the wariness in her narrowed eyes. "Whether you recognise it or not, it has your name on it, so you should do the honours."

Steeling herself against the plethora of booby traps her

imagination paraded past – from stupid sprung snakes to IED's – Jen clicked the two latches. If she'd been on her own, she might have opened it an inch and shone her phone torch in to check for wires, but they were already way too suspicious.

"Come on, love, it won't bite. Don't keep us in suspenders."

Hearing one of her gran's old sayings gave her comfort, and she raised the lid, recognising the shiny blue rock-and-roll skirt she'd worn for the Queen's Platinum Jubilee party, along with a bolero cardigan.

Vickie gasped. "Oohhh, that's gorgeous."

Spotting other clothes from the rack in the attic, cogs started to whirl. Isaac. *Questioning her*. But the two women wore matching quizzical expressions, so she nodded. "Yes, these are my things. Oh dear." She sank back into the seat as an idea formed.

"You've gone as white as a sheet. What happened?"

"It's starting to come back now. My boyfriend bought the tickets and booked a room – presumably with you?"

Dora's hand shot up to cover her mouth. "Of course. That's why the name sounded familiar. But you're not booked in until Thursday. The thirtieth. I thought it was a bit strange, because he said it was for the second week, but there'll only be a couple of days left as it all finishes on Saturday the second."

"You mean it's not Thursday the thirtieth today?"

"No love. It's Monday the twenty seventh." A frown.

Jen's smile wasn't fooling anyone. "Of course it is."

Dora peered, her face severe. "What really happened?"

"Honestly? I'm not sure. The last thing I remember was getting on the train – no, wait. I chatted to a girl about how excited I was to be watching the matches. The next thing I knew was waking up on a bench in the park and a kind lady called Betty making me a cup of tea."

"That'll be Betty Cartwright. Lovely lady." *Or not.*

Vickie's derisive snort was rewarded with a glare as Dora folded her arms. "Well that settles it. That girl probably had an accomplice and they stole your case to get at the tickets. You must have said they were in there."

Jen beetled her eyebrows, trying to follow her reasoning, while a teeny-tiny part of her felt as though Dora was almost like an NPC feeding convenient lines to move the story on. "But why would they return the case?"

Dora scoffed. "Maybe they had a shred of decency in them, who knows. Just be grateful you got your things back. But it's all worked out well in the end. I have tickets for the rest of the week – you must have them."

"And don't even think of refusing. After what you've been through, it's the least we can do." Vickie smiled. Then, with a gasp, she shot up. "I promised Shirley I'd help; she's facing a Norwegian girl with a really long first serve tomorrow. She has a practice court booked at two."

Dora glanced at the clock. "You'd best get a move on if you don't want to let her down."

"I need to change, and I'm sure you'd like to freshen up. Shall I show you to your room?"

Jen nodded, thrusting everything back in the case and snapping it shut. She carried it to the first floor where room thirteen turned out to be a double with a small vanity unit in the corner and a mirrored cupboard over the washbasin.

"This is wonderful, thank you."

"The bathroom's just down the hall if you need to pee."

"Thank you." She opened the case on the bed and hung up a couple of the dresses in the small wardrobe to encourage the creases to drop out.

Whoever had sorted it – and her best guess had to be Isaac – had packed light, and the small soap bag had genuine-looking items from the fifties. In amongst them, folded over several times, was a large yellow post-it note.

When she got to the last fold, she spotted her name and, recognising the scrawl, she unfolded it and read:

Dear Jen,

If you're reading this then you have travelled back in time to 1955 and are currently with your gran and great gran. Please don't be angry with me – I thought you might appreciate spending some time with your relatives. Maybe you can finally get to the bottom of the real reason why Victoria gave up her promising tennis career.

I hope you can forgive my shenanigans enough to enjoy your trip to the past – it's the kind of holiday few people get to experience. I will be along when the tournament ends to guide you back.

With love

    Isaac

    xxx

A knock on the door had her shoving it into her handbag and she ran to join her teenage gran.

Ch 11 – Siege and More Spies

Cursed Castle

The jester clapped his hands. "So, it's time to move on. I suggest you use torches as it will be dark outside. And take care as we return to the gatehouse – stick to the paths as the grass may be slippery and the slopes can take you by surprise."

Setting off at a cracking pace, the bells on his hat jingling, he paid no attention as the others had to scurry to keep up with him. He didn't slow the pace as they climbed the circular staircase to the top of the tower, so they were quite dizzy and out of breath when they reached the top.

They fetched out into the open air and he chortled. "I strongly advise you not to go too close to the edge, it's quite a drop to the bottom, and there's no water in the moat to soften your fall."

Rosalina glared at him. "There was no need to drag us along at such a punishing pace. You're nothing but a sadist."

"Sticks and stones may break my bones, but names will never hurt me." His sing-song tone disappeared as he got up close and personal so his spittle hit her face. "Scared, are we? Angry? Or just out of breath? Whichever way, your blood is dashing around and your heart is beating in the same way as the poor souls who had to stand here waiting for whatever the marauding attackers threw at them. Literally." He slipped onto one of the crenel spaces between the merlons in the parapet, and seconds later, they were bombarded by the ear-splitting sounds of marching feet, clanking armour and war cries.

All three covered their ears with their hands until it stopped, leaving behind a silence which rang loud.

The jester set the scene for this latest hunt. "In1642, Charles the First had fallen out with his parliament about who held ultimate authority because he believed in the 'divine rights of kings.' Each side refused to concede to the others point of view."

Kurt yawned loudly, and the jester rounded on him. "Are we keeping you up, Mr Small? Nearly done here."

He struck a pose, setting off the bells on his hat. Where was I before I was so rudely interrupted? Ah yes. You may know the extravagantly-dressed royalists as Cavaliers – which suited them in every sense of the word. The other side, known as Roundheads, were the opposite: parsimonious, puritanical parliamentarians."

Kurt made winding on motions with his hand. "Why you imagine we need a history lesson is beyond me. As is why you think *you* can teach *us!* Get to the point, man."

"This point, Mr Rude?" A short sword appeared in the jester's hand, its point inches away from Kurt's face.

"Point taken. We're in a castle surrounded by weapons." With surprising cool, the German pushed the blade away as the jester continued.

"And that's exactly what happened here. The castle and titles had been inherited by Robert Greville, a radical puritan activist and vociferous critic of the king."

Both Kurt and Grenville opened their mouths, shutting them again at his toxic glare.

"Unbeknown to him, a Cavalier spy had infiltrated at a

high position, sending out details of weapons and food shipments and useful information how to target the castle's defences."

Rosalina stiffened. "This is where they cornered him. Someone's coming through." A piercing cackle preceded the most vile voice yet. "Beware the grey dandy – he'll slit your throat as soon as look at you."

"STOP HIM! Saxon's a spy." A shout came up from the lower floor, followed by a commotion of thumps, clanks and screams which suggested someone had fallen down the stairs. Or been pushed …

Heavy footsteps on the stairs heralded the appearance of a heavyset man in the dull roundhead uniform, and they watched as he slammed the door and barred it.

Grenville stood in front to block his path.

"Out of my way."

"No. We need–" But the professor's request was curtailed as the man grabbed his jacket and forced him against the wall.

"You *need* to let me pass."

Rosalina screeched, pointing a finger. "There's the Cavalier spy. He's up here."

"Shut up, witch." He shoved Grenville so hard he lost his footing and toppled backwards, scrabbling for a hold on the stone merlons as he fell between them.

Kurt moved with surprising speed, hauling him back so hard he fell to the ground, coughing and whimpering.

Meanwhile, Saxon grabbed the possessed girl, wielding a knife and telling them all to stay back or he would slice her neck.

Grenville stirred himself, reaching out, but dizziness overtook him. This was not on at all – the poor girl had barely had time to recover from the previous attempt on her life. As he tried to lift himself up, the spy seemed to tune into his intention and brandished the knife in his direction.

With no regard for his safety, Kurt stepped forward. "Let her go – she's no threat to you."

"That's as maybe, but she's interfered once too often, and if you're all trying to save her, you won't be after me."

As he raised his knife-hand to make good his threat, the stable-boy came at him from behind, throwing himself at them with such force Rosalina was released. She ran into Kurt's arms and he sheltered her as she buried her head into his shoulder.

In the tussle, Tom and Saxon slammed each other against the walls, but the spy retained his grip on the knife which cared not who it slashed as they bounced around, snarling and grunting. Being older and much heavier, Saxon managed to shove him down onto one of the crenel spaces, trying to force his body over the edge. In a move too quick for anyone watching to anticipate, the brave lad thrust his knee in the man's groin. As he bucked in pain, Tom grabbed his shoulders and kicked against the ground. The pair of them toppled backwards, falling arse-over-tit, bouncing off the ramparts and crashing to the ground.

Shock at such selfless courage stunned them all into silence which Kurt broke with characteristic insensitivity. "I had grave suspicions about that character from the start, but when I checked, M is not one of the third letters, so maybe I misjudged him."

Grenville spoke up. "I had similar misgivings about those stable lads both looking the same."

The jester giggled. "It may interest you to know that the spot on the ramparts where they bounced was exactly the same spot where Dan Bloxham dumped the body of his Pol into the river."

Rosalina gasped. "I *knew* Tom was lying about that, but why? What's the connection?"

Taking out his notebook, Grenville flipped to a page of scribbles. "I got as far as separating Blackshaw into Blacks and haw. If you change the A to an O, you have Blocks."

"Or Blox." Rosalina squealed. "And if you invert the letter W it becomes an M."

"Blocks and ham is Bloxham. Very clever." Kurt inclined his head.

"But not clever enough, and a little too late." Grenville grimaced.

"Dan ends in N which sits next to M – a double letter. I can definitely believe *he* was the big bad." Rosalina clutched her neck. "Or at least, in his service."

"Well done, hunters. You've made real progress today." The jester tinkled his bells.

Ch 12 – An Extraordinary Holiday

June 1955

Jen marvelled at the difference to her world as they walked the few hundred yards, with Vickie rattling on about how it was a poor show this year. Of the ten British women in her draw, only two made it through to the third round where they both lost. "My friend Laura, was knocked out in straight sets by her mate Rita. It's always hard when that happens."

"I imagine there's quite a lot of rivalry between you."

"Only on the court. Off court, we all help each other. Laura won the girls title twice, and she was really kind to me when I qualified the following year – she's the reason I got through to the semis that year."

"Which is why you want to help Shirley."

"Exactly. The Yanks call it buddying up."

"Where I come from, we call it mentoring – when an experienced person helps a newcomer."

"Not as fun as being a buddy." She blushed.

"You like the – Yanks? Aren't they super-competitive?"

"Their coaches certainly are. I thought ours were bad enough, but …" She glanced away. "Anyway, whatever their methods, it works – they have five of the top six seeds. Apart from Angie M, who got knocked out in the second round by a Hungarian, the quarterfinals are exactly as the draw would place them."

Jen chuckled. "Don't be surprised if we get an All-American semi-final."

"Aww – I'd love to see Angie B make the final, she's

on great form – only lost one set so far and after that, her opponent seemed to give up. Another Yank."

Jen couldn't decide whether Vickie admired or disliked the Americans, sometimes she'd use the term casually, other times with affection. But never derogatory – it wasn't intentionally racist, simply a hangover from the war.

The queue at the entrance chattered about someone fainting in the heat. Vickie seemed quite agitated about the proposed wait, and tugged on her arm. "Come on, we'll go in the players entrance, I can't wait here."

"But I won't have the right pass."

"Don't worry, I'll get you in. There have to be some perks to being a reigning champion."

Minutes later, the reason for her haste was revealed as she ducked into the ladies like a girl on a mission. Jen followed a little slower, but the noises she heard on entering were disturbing to say the least. She called through. "Vickie, are you all right, love?" How weird did that feel? Calling her grandmother "love" in role-reversal stranger than anything she'd seen in a movie.

"Yes. I – I'm fine. Won't be a tick." When she emerged, she dashed to the sink and treated her hands to a wash more thorough than any scrub nurse.

"Is something wrong?"

"Why do you ask?"

"That kind of explosive pooing can indicate intolerance to certain types of food. Do you get it often?"

She stared at the floor, blushing furiously and Jen realised this was not a topic teenage girls of any age felt comfortable discussing. "Sorry. I didn't mean to embarrass

126

you, but if it happens every time you eat cake, for example, a food allergy can easily be diagnosed and treated."

"You mean go to the doctors? I couldn't talk to a man about this; I simply couldn't. I'd die of shame."

"Please don't upset yourself." *Time to back off.* "Will you be all right to play against Shirley?"

"Sure. I'll be fine. You don't have to come, you should go to centre court – they'll be doing the quarter finals."

"I'd rather come with you – if you wouldn't mind."

"To keep an eye on me?" She bristled.

Bugger that. "Are you kidding? The only chance I'll ever have to go behind the scenes at Wimbledon? I wouldn't miss it for the world."

Grinning, Vickie took her hand and pulled her out of the rooms, dashing through the crowds to reach the practice courts just after two where an anxious girl stood, spinning her racquet in her hand.

"There you are." She flung her arms around her. "I thought you'd deserted me."

"Sorry. You'll have to blame me, I slowed Vickie down. Not as fit as I thought." Jen stuck out her hand. "I'm Jen. A … friend of the family."

Vickie hugged her arm. "You're being modest, Auntie Jen. You run faster than most thirty-year-olds I know."

Shirley scoffed. "I *should* say she doesn't know many flirty thirties, but she can't get away from them." A wink.

"What are you standing around chatting for?" Vickie unzipped her racquet case. "We only have an hour."

Sitting at the net, her finger on the cord like a professional, Jen relished the sight of her gran at her peak, darting around the court. Her white skirt, although higher on the knee than those in the pictures, was nothing like as short as the modern players. Although she was biased, Jen couldn't help comparing the two girls – Vickie definitely had an X-factor which escaped Shirley, who looked more homely.

Two lads who'd been practicing a few courts down stopped on their way past, openly admiring her, while barely glancing at Shirley, and they hadn't even noticed Jen, who would have been obscured by the net.

"You're leaning too far back. I'll show you." The older of the lads, who obviously fancied himself as an expert, came up behind Vickie, but she wriggled out of his grasp.

"Because I'm trying to hit long serves like Shirley's opponent tomorrow."

"You won't do it like that. Watch." He talked through each of the steps as he demonstrated.

Jen had to bite her tongue as she imagined both girls knew everything he mentioned about placing the ball, shoulder positioning and powering from the legs. Finally she'd had enough and stood. "I know you're trying to help, but Shirley doesn't have long. It would be far more useful if you could give her a few long serves to practice on."

He jumped back, his tone dismissive. "Who are you?"

"Someone who has Shirley's best interests at heart."

"She's right, Bob. Here, Shirley, let me have a go." The other lad strode up to the baseline and Vickie skipped out of the way, dragging Bob with her.

They watched as the dark-haired lad directed several serves to Shirley's forehand, then to her backhand. They all spotted she was standing too far over in an attempt to favour her forehand, leaving the court wide open.

"But Mark, I daren't – my backhand's so weak."

"Then maybe we should work on that instead." He smiled at her.

An approaching couple walked past to take the court the boys had just vacated. Mark suggested they stayed until someone kicked them off, but no-one did, so they had an extra hour with all three of them analysing Shirley's play and making subtle improvements.

Captivated by their generosity, Jen watched in delight as they ended with an impromptu mixed doubles set which attracted a few more onlookers as they showed off great teamwork skills. She figured this wasn't the first time they'd played as a foursome, and Bob was obviously the most experienced, being a couple of years older.

As the four shook hands after calling it a tie, a man with a professional camera snapped the moment.

"Would you mind posing together, the four of you? Two junior champs and their protégées will make a lovely shot for the article I'm writing to inspire British hopefuls."

They moved as directed and Bob nodded at the camera. "Just so long as you're not going to use it for anything dubious. Coach would have our guts for garters."

"Absolutely not." He clicked. "And maybe another–"

Jen's eye's narrowed as a vague memory surfaced – something about her gran being taken advantage of by the press. She marched up, deliberately photo-bombing. "I think you've had more than enough. Any further requests should go through the press office. You know you're not supposed to take anything which hasn't been approved."

"All right, love. Keep your wig on." He scuttled off, no doubt seeking other unsuspecting victims.

"Wow, Auntie Jen, that was impressive. I think you scared him off with all that talk about rules."

"This is your aunt?" Bob's mock grimace was comical. "I'm so sorry. I should have spotted the resemblance straight away. Please forgive my earlier rudeness."

Jen waved it away. "It's obvious you know your stuff, but so do these girls. Learn to pitch to your audience and don't assume they know nothing. After all, Vickie did win last year."

"You're completely right. I'm sorry Vic, if I came across as pompous. I'll try harder next time."

"No you won't because it will all have gone in one ear and out the other as usual."

As everyone nodded, he held his hands up. "You got me bang to rights. I am who I am."

Vickie squeezed his arm. "But we still love you anyway. Come on guys, I need some barley squash."

For a while, Jen forgot about her predicament, happy to – how had Isaac put it? Have a holiday in her family's past.

After a pleasant evening getting to know her family, the following day brought more singular experiences as she watched the last senior Brit knocked out of the singles in straight sets.

That evening, browsing through the bookshelf in the parlour, she spotted a familiar name on a book called *Life's Ebb and Flow* – by Frances Evelyn Maynard Greville,

Countess of Warwick. *Daisy*. She peeked inside to confirm.

Dora called her over. "What do you have there?" On seeing the book, she chuckled. "She's one of Vickie's heroines. Can't say I cared for the book myself – a bit too hifalutin for my tastes. But she's inspired Vickie into thinking about life after the few years she'll be young and fit enough to compete."

"That's good. What does she want to do? Coaching?"

"Nothing so ordinary. She has visions of using her success to encourage girls to take up sports and compete in same arena as men. I've tried to suggest that Daisy could only do what she did because she had so much money …"

"But you don't want to run her life."

"Exactly. She has to be free to make her own mistakes."

By Wednesday, Jen was in the swing, planning out the matches she could watch, designing her viewing around the All-American ladies semi-final and the two men's singles quarter-finals, catching at least a set from each one.

She couldn't deny finding the men's matches more exciting, and marvelled at the difference in the two Americans' styles. Joe's stylish serve-and-volley game showed exactly why he was the number one seed, but Vickie and Shirley were most interested in his impressive one-handed backhand, trying to learn from it. The court filled up for the next match – Freddie's Hollywood leading-man good looks guaranteed lots of female fans. But his smooth ground strokes and consistency had the men cheering as all three sets went to a single service break.

Shirley and Mark both got through their quarter-final

junior matches, and Vickie invited Jen to an impromptu dinner to celebrate. Having been knocked out in the third round of the seniors, Bob declined the invitation, claiming he didn't want to rain on their parade. Vickie had more than enough excitement to make up for his absence as they met her friends at a local restaurant.

When they got there, Jen was thrilled to spot Joe and Freddie on the next table. Apparently, Joe's wife, Shauna had gone to bed with a migraine, and Jen sympathised, immediately drawn to his shy humility. Although not as obviously good-looking as Freddie, he had a wholesome, all-American openness which she found endearing.

Freddie however, debonair in a tailored jacket and elegant tie, knew exactly how to wind everyone around his little finger. Without consulting anyone, he got Joe to help him push their tables together and ordered champagne all round. After toasting everyone's successes, he grimaced, nudging Joe. "Well, I suspect that's it for me for another year. No one's getting past this machine."

Jen knew fishing when she saw it. "You certainly won't with that attitude."

"Ouch. I deserved that." Everyone agreed as Vickie toasted to his skill at charming everyone but his opponents.

Jen found herself trying to make amends. "I read somewhere Wimbledon was your favourite event.

He grinned. "Because it had the best grass courts in the world? Yep, it's the one thing they always quote about me over here." He winked. "I also said England has the prettiest girls, but that never makes it to print."

Joe chuckled. "That's because all those New England

mammas are hoping you'll come back across the pond and marry one of their debutantes."

He scoffed. "Sorry, but I can't see that happening. Europe's much more my style." He glanced at Jen. "I bet you've been to Paris, so you'll know what I mean about walking along the Seine at night."

She smiled. "Mais oui, monsieur. Très jolie."

"See Joe – the women over here are all so well-travelled and educated."

"Shauna has travelled. To Hawaii."

"Sure, on honeymoon. But technically it's still in the good old US of A. I bet she never even had a passport before then." At Joe's shrug, Freddie relented. "Anyway, she's smart and funny as well as an ex-beauty queen, so you struck real lucky."

The banter continued, and Jen couldn't help but notice how Freddie monopolised Vickie, leaving her chatting to Joe, one of her gran's all-time heroes. *Strange how she didn't remember her gran ever mentioning Freddie with the same affection.*

On Thursday, watching the first set of the gentlemen's semi-finals, Jen felt so much more engaged, and actually thanked Isaac for making this unique experience possible. Knowing a little of the personalities involved, she smiled at a loud woman in the next row declaring it a grudge match and pontificating about how much the men disliked each other. *If only she'd seen them last night, teasing and joking.*

But all hints of smiles were gone as their on-the-dour-side-of-neutral expressions gave nothing away. Every game went to serve, and it got to 7-6 before Joe finally broke through, but only after conceding a couple of set points. He was indeed serving like a machine, with so many unreturnable aces, but many of Freddie's service games had gone to several deuces, making it a long set.

Vickie seemed unusually invested, several times shouting encouragement, and he made a point of making sure a number of the kisses he blew into the audience were aimed at her. But his statement last night had been prophetic as he only held serve twice in the next two sets, giving Joe a three-set win.

As they hustled to the ladies before dashing across to number 1 court for Shirley's semi-final, Jen heard strange noises from the next cubicle. At first she thought it was a wail, but couldn't decide whether there was relief – maybe even laughter in there. "Everything okay in there?"

"Um, yes. It's just the curse."

Jen searched for a vending machine but of course, there were none. As she racked her brain for whether tampons had been invented yet, Vickie came out, all smiles.

"Thank goodness Laura told me always to carry a couple of tampons and clean panties. If it catches you in the middle of a game, it can be horrendous. I'm sure you can imagine how it would look on court – they didn't take it into account when they decreed all garments must be white." She giggled, depositing the packaging in the bin and washing her hands. "Not that I've had to worry, it's been months since – oh." Her hands flew up to her face, and then reached out, imploring. "Please don't tell Mum."

"You mean …?" Jen's eyes widened at the implication, trying not to judge. *No wonder she was so relieved.* But no period for so long could mean a miscarriage. She had to probe, trying to be casual. "How many months?"

"I don't know. Nine or ten – maybe longer. They've been irregular for years."

"Really?" It didn't stack up.

"What? Why are you frowning so hard?" A beat, followed by outrageous laughter. "I get it. You think I suspected I was pregnant? Shame on you."

"I'm sorry, it was just you were so – relieved when it came. It's a natural reaction, after all you're old enough–"

"But I'm not that sort of girl and I'm horrified you thought I might be." Tears sprang to her eyes and, with a sniff, she spun away.

Tact was never Jen's forte. "Someone as gorgeous as you is bound to attract a lot of male attention – no matter what their age. It's inevitable that they will try it on. My concern was someone had maybe forced–"

She sobbed and her whole body shuddered.

Catching her arm, Jen gently tugged her around, softening her tone. "What happened? Is it something to do with one of the boys?"

The sobbing stepped up a gear and she didn't resist as Jen pulled her into a loose hug, stroking her back.

"Oh Auntie Jen, I didn't mean to. It was only once–"

"Shhh. No one's judging. These things happen. Was it Bob? He seems very taken with you. Or Mark?"

"If only. It was …" She wiped the tears, her tone dark with anger. "It doesn't matter. I was nothing but a notch on his bedpost. He's collecting champions, can you believe?" A snort. "He's not even very good. Not that I'd know any

135

better – he took my virginity and it meant nothing to him."

The incident took the shine off the rest of the day and she was barely aware of Shirley's easy victory as her mind itemised the clues to uncover the true story. It hinged around Vickie's obsession with the Americans. Firstly, the obvious candidate for the pregnancy scare was Freddie, but Jen needed more data before pursuing that possibility. Her reaction suggested Vickie would not be risking a reoccurrence, so it was not the most pressing issue.

Jen's own bulimia experience had led to arming herself with as much information as possible and, while Vickie was by no means a textbook case, there were more than sufficient hints. Although she'd shown no overt reluctance to the massive wedge of cake, Jen recognised the micro-tells in flaring eyes and slight hesitation before each mouthful as though gearing herself up to face an unpleasant task. This was immediately followed by the aftermath of a laxative – no mistaking that noise.

Jen had picked up enough from the girls' chatter to spot how the American coaches placed great emphasis on body shape, wanting players to look slim and glamorous to gain support from crowd and ultimately sponsors. *Hence the availability of laxatives.* Vickie had mentioned how her previous coach had limited her diet and over-trained, which would account for the missed periods. The new coach, although much better, had mostly coached men. His main aim involved getting her to partner with his star pupil, Mark, for mixed doubles, calling them his golden couple.

As though peer-pressure and poor training weren't bad enough, Jen knew "ugly parents" ramped up the stresslevels. She grinned at the un-PC term for those who tried to live vicariously through their children's achievements. Although Dora was nothing like as demanding, she nevertheless added pressure in her pride and desperation for success at one end and over-feeding on the other. Add in Vickie's performance anxiety and Virgo perfectionism, and an eating disorder became a given.

She'd hoped to have a chat with Vickie that evening, but Isaac chose that point to turn up unannounced. Walking through the door, she heard the male voice and dashed in to see him sitting in the chair by Dora's sofa. "*Darling*. I wasn't expecting you for a couple of days."

Ch 13 – Unexpected Journey

June 1955/2022

He stood, embracing her awkwardly. "I know, but something came up at work. You know how temperamental the device can be. We may have to leave a little earlier."

"Not before the final, surely?" Vickie seemed upset.

"If they must go, they must go. Some things are more important than tennis." Dora tapped the side of her nose. "And now, young lady, will you set the table? I've ordered a fish supper from the chippy and it will be here shortly."

Vickie's eyes widened. "You got Browning to deliver?"

A snort. "*Behave yourself.* Billy from next door went on his bicycle for sixpence." She smiled at Isaac. "Would you like to go and wash up? Jen will show you the bathroom."

"Thank you, you're too kind." Isaac picked up a smaller version of the case he'd packed for her, and Jen led him to her room, wondering how the evening would pan out.

Once inside, he closed the door and bent down on one knee. "Please forgive me, Jen. I know what I did was despicable, but I promise, I only wanted to do something good for you. By the way they've accepted you, it seems your adventure hasn't been all bad."

Although she'd had plenty of time to ponder on her reaction when he finally appeared, events had been so distracting she hadn't prepared a speech. "No matter your intentions, there's no excuse for the way you did it, and for that I can't forgive you. Ever. How dare you imagine you can use me as a lab rat without my permission?"

"Because if I'd asked, you'd have said no, and missed a

once-in-a-lifetime opportunity. If I'd had more time–"

"Why did it have to be then?"

"Because it's all tied in with the master numbers. Being thirty-three in twenty-two–"

"Except I'm only thirty two."

"What? Why didn't I know that? Explains so much."

"How do you mean?"

"I can't elaborate right now for fear of mucking up the delicate balance. Can you have faith for a little while longer? It will all come out as soon as I've secured the last few parts of the puzzle, I promise."

She folded her arms. "That's not going to wash. You've done nothing to earn my faith, and what with the spy cameras and everything, I can't trust a word you say."

He closed his eyes, breathing deeply. Then they shot open, and he clutched her arms. "You know Georgie's always going on about the power of thought?"

She shrugged him off with a scowl. "It's not just her. Ever since that 'Secret' book came out in the early noughties, people have been using it all over the world."

He frowned. "How's that possible if it's a secret?"

She slid a glance, trying to spot if he was winding her up. But Isaac didn't do irony, much less teasing. *At least, the old Isaac didn't*. "The law of attraction?"

"Right. I think. But anyway, time-travelling is tied to deep-seated instincts, and too much information will skew the results. That's my best guess until I know more."

"Send more guinea pigs with no warning, you mean?"

He glanced down to the right. "Something like that."

Jen hadn't kept up with the research about non-verbal

cues, but his fidgeting hands suggested a lack of truth. *Or it could just be an OCD tic.* But she had few alternatives.

A discreet tap on the door called them to dinner, where she watched an alien version of her socially-inept landlord lay on a level of charm which could only have developed from their interactions as Kurt and Evadne. *Or maybe from watching Ben playing romantic roles.* Whatever the source, the two women lapped it up and she overheard Dora raving about the wonderful match they made.

When it came time for bed, Dora glared at Isaac. "I would never normally countenance the idea of an unmarried couple sharing a bedroom. If you'd been clearer when you booked–"

"Apologies, but you'd already said you only had double rooms left. I can go somewhere else if you'd rather."

"Where might you find a bed on the eve of the finals?"

"I could sleep down here on the couch."

"There's barely room for me. I can't get up the stairs. No, I'll relax my rules just this once." She wagged a finger. "But make sure you keep the noise down." A chuckle.

"I can assure you, Mrs Potts, there won't be a sound." He blushed and Jen saw her and Vickie exchange a melting glance. *If only they knew.*

"Awkward or what?" She whispered into his ear as they exited the room, and he put his arm around her shoulders, chuckling at the almost-clucking sounds following them out of the door.

"Might as well put on the show they're expecting." He nuzzled her hair, and held her hand as they ascended.

The unexpected softness of his fingers against hers

caused a weird sensation Jen couldn't have diagnosed if her life depended on it. Peeking at his enigma-crossed-with-a-puzzle expression, she speculated how he might deal with the impossible situation in front of them. All the guests in the nearby rooms were early risers, and she'd never heard a peep out of any of them. She suspected they all worked in the city but lived in the country as they'd all finished breakfast and were on trains by the time she wandered in for the last sitting of the day.

His solution involved a rolled up blanket down the middle of the bed, which worked fine for her. After ascertaining she didn't want to go back the following day, he suggested she should use the bathroom first.

On her return, he was in bed, the minty smell evidence he'd cleaned his teeth in the small washbasin. The gentle snore sounded artificial, and she sensed his consciousness in the room. If he wanted to feign sleep, she didn't mind, she had no urge to spend more time discussing the wrongs or rights of his behaviour – what was done, was done. *Get over it*. More pressing was the need to fix her gran's problems, and her mind pounced on the awkwardness between her and Isaac, comparing it to Vickie and Freddie.

When she replayed their behaviour, she was 99% convinced he hadn't bedded her because of the lack of intimate gestures which bonded a sexually active couple. Although he loved to flirt, she sensed a strong core of decency which suggested he wouldn't boast about bedpost-notches. And she couldn't imagine Joe being such close friends with someone who would. In many ways, the pair reminded her of Ben and Kev – the studious gentleman and the lady-killing trickster. But thoughts of them weren't going to reveal the true villain of the piece. It would be a tad more awkward to get to the bottom of the mystery with Isaac there, but she prayed for an opportunity tomorrow.

It came from an unexpected quarter at the end of the girls' singles final, where Shirley had a straight-set win over her French opponent. Vickie was ecstatic and, when she was called down to attend the award ceremony, her friend Laura sat in her seat, her face serious.

"Hello, Jen. You don't know me, but Vickie's told me so much about you, I feel I know you."

"All bad, I hope?" Jen's eyes sparkled as she trotted out the age-old rejoinder.

Laura blinked as though she'd never heard it, which was likely – in 1955, it wouldn't have been used often enough to become a trope. "No, I assure you."

Jen smiled. "Ignore me. Just a joke. How can I help?"

"I'm worried about Vickie."

"Because of the Americans?"

"She told you about them? Well that's a step in the right direction."

"I suspect she didn't tell me everything, but I imagine they encouraged her to make herself sick."

"I only caught her doing it once. Thankfully, once they're gone she won't be as influenced by such rubbish."

"I know from personal experience it's easy to get hooked. And she's taken a step further in using a laxative."

"No. when?"

As Jen swapped details with Laura, she felt encouraged by the girl's grasp of the situation, if not a little shocked by her casual attitude to using suppositories. She slid a glance. "You don't know if she's still seeing that guy?"

"The one who got her … oops." she clutched her mouth.

"He didn't. I believe her lack of periods was caused by overtraining and undereating."

"That's a relief. About the pregnancy. Not the rest."

"You didn't answer my question."

"About the jerk? He's well out of the picture. As soon as he had what he wanted, he was off. Thankfully."

"So there's no chance she'd ever–"

"Never. He was out in the second round and shipped straight back to the States."

"So it wasn't Freddie, then?" *She had to know for sure.*

A tinkly laugh. "Freddie?" She lowered her tone as people glared. "Never. He's a sweetheart. I know he comes off as a smooth charmer, but deep down he's quite shy."

The officials had finished laying the carpet for the awards, and they watched with pride as the young champion received her trophy. A runner came to fetch Laura, saying the press wanted pictures of the three British junior champs in the past five years.

This gave Jen a moment alone to ponder on how to approach the topic with Vickie. At least her brief liaison with a much older man would remain just that. Jen had to respect her desire to suppress the unpleasant memories, and felt it her duty as honorary aunt to pass on the tie-cutting exercises Georgie had taught.

While Jen had the privileged ticket into the player's family area, Isaac had been content to wander around, absorbing the bygone atmosphere. They sat together to

143

watch the all-Australian gentleman's doubles final, and she chuckled at his fair attempt at the cut-glass vowels and more precise speech of the period. But his credible performance in the role of solicitous boyfriend surprised her most. If she didn't know better, she would totally have been fooled into thinking the tender glances and chivalrous gestures were for real.

From the start, their relationship had been checkered: mostly his self-absorption and failure to observe the most basic social niceties had exasperated the bejaysus out of her. But recently, she'd been surprised by his attention and wondered if this was his version of the mating dance. It was a tricky one, and her gentle heart wouldn't allow her to reject his clumsy advances. Not that she'd encouraged him, just retained a pleasant neutrality.

"Penny for 'em?" His proximity as he leaned to whisper startled her. He gestured at the match. "They're clearly not holding your attention. Are you all tennised out?"

Blinking, she sought a cover story. "I was just wondering what the others were doing – and what reason you gave for being away."

"It was easy. Kev got three tickets to see the Dragon slayer evening show so Ben and Georgie are spending the day exploring the bits of the castle they missed last time."

"While you did your knight in shining armour bit to rescue this damsel in distress." She grinned.

"Hardly. You're definitely the antithesis of helpless, and I'm no KiSA. You did read my note, didn't you?"

"Only after I'd spent a while trying to figure it all out. Some notice would have been nice."

"I can't apologise enough."

"You can try."

He moved to bend down on one knee, and she hissed.

"Don't do that here, people will think you're proposing." Yet again, he'd out-manoeuvred her. *Brat*.

"I'm sorry. And I'm truly sorry for not consulting you. It really was all about timing – things came together in such a rush, which is why I took the day off to experiment."

"But the timing was off – I left 2022 in Thursday 30th and turned up here on Monday 27th – or was it deliberate?"

"If only. I'd got the date wrong because I didn't realise they moved the competition forward a week to give three weeks after the French Open, so people got a longer rest. I'd intended for you to arrive on the thirtieth, so I need to address that glitch."

"So how do we get back?"

He explained how Eric made several sets of dice and he had a theory that each pair imprints on the first person to use them. "So I've brought your dice, along with the pair I've been using to travel back here and set things up. I'm hoping we can both travel on my pair, but if not, yours should get you back safely."

A huge gasp had them watching the court as one of the Aussies fell over while managing to return a killing lob and somehow his partner kept the ball in play long enough for him to bounce up and return to the net for a quick-fire volley sequence which lasted over a dozen shots before the other side slammed it into the top of the net. Even then the top-spin had it curling over and dropping. A superhuman lunge had him getting to it with just enough slice to trickle it back over and win the point.

The applause deafened as everyone jumped to their feet, and the umpire tried three times before getting sufficient silence to announce the score.

When they got back to the house, Dora was in a strange mood after a visit from the doctor. "The results of the blood tests have come back, and they show a bone deficiency. Apparently it's quite common after the war because people couldn't get the right foods. Osteo-something or other."

"Osteoporosis? Osteoarthritis?" Isaac jumped in.

"The first one. How do you know about it?"

"My – um – sister suffered from it." He shot a 'help' glance at Jen. It was too good a chance to miss.

"She was a brilliant athlete, but she overdid her training and ended up missing her periods for over a year. The disruption to her hormones weakened her bones so she had to give it up."

Dora peered at Vickie. "Well that hasn't happened to you, has it?"

With a sob, she ran up to her room, and Jen assured Dora she would get to the bottom of it.

She opened the door on the first tap and flung herself in Jen's arms. "Oh, Auntie Jen what do I do?"

Realising the majority of her fear came from the idea of telling Dora she was no longer a virgin, Jen teased it out of her bit by bit. "How could I admit to Mum the possibility I might be pregnant?"

"But the lack of periods went on long before you slept with him, so why didn't you say anything then?"

"Because all the girls were the same – it was normal."

"Then that's what you tell her. The truth is always best."

"But she'll wonder why I ran off."

"Because you were ashamed of not telling her."

"I never actually lied about it."

"Then you have nothing to fear. And actually, Dora is a lot more understanding than you might think."

She nodded. "I saw how she saw with you and Isaac."

It seemed the perfect opportunity to delve into all the other things related to the eating disorder, and share her own experience, and she finished off showing her the tie-cutting technique to rid herself of the entire incident.

When they went back down, Dora was singing. "… three for a girl and four for a boy." She peered at Vickie then explained how she'd spotted four magpies on the day he'd shown up, and three of the black and white birds before Jen appeared. She sang the entire verse.

Somehow, Isaac managed to smooth everything so their departure before watching the final seemed the only possible solution. Jen was relieved her gran seemed in a much better place mentally, and the bond with her mother had strengthened after Vickie's tearful confession.

Sitting on the same bench she'd woken up on, Jen took a second to decide when she'd like to return in 2022 – before or after the second week's matches. As he'd surmised, she was all tennised out and really didn't need to spend a week in the modern championship, which could only be a cardboard facsimile of the fabulous 1955 experience. She understood the need for discretion and followed him into a clump of bushes, pleased to find herself back in the attic with a couple of hours before the gang returned. More than enough time to come up with a cover story involving suspicion of Covid at her cousin's house, but negative tests in London and back home. Isaac's acceptance of her immunity helped, but the others still huddled on the opposite sofa while they all swapped tales.

After listening to their thrilling accounts of the live-action show with Guy of Warwick defeating dragons, Jen admitted to working on the riddle.

"It wasn't Isaac's fault, I tricked him into revealing it."

He frowned. "But you seemed to know it."

She shrugged. "What can I say? I saw some of Kev's early doodles, and I do love a riddle. The second clue, 'not steady' screamed anagram to me, but after getting nowhere with every possible combination, I tried a few synonyms of steady and came up with the perfect word. Apart from the fact it had a couple of extra letters – TT."

Georgie got in first. "As in Time Tower. Which one was that?" She glanced at Kev who remained impassive. "I remember: it was the Watergate one with the chap who got murdered. Sounds like potential for revenge."

Ben got really excited. "It could link to the TT races – something to do with the Isle of Man? I swear I saw the flag somewhere in the castle."

Georgie frowned. "How does that help? Isn't it some kind of three-legged thing?"

Isaac sniffed. "At risk of sounding even more Sheldon than normal, a triskelion is a symbol consisting of three protrusions with threefold symmetry."

"Your point being?" Ben, Jen and Georgie chorused,

almost in harmony.

"In the case of this flag, the protrusions are armour-clad legs with spurs. Perfectly at home in a castle. Maybe it's pointing us to the armoury."

They all peered at Kev. Chuckling, he wagged a finger. "Whereas I can't fault the enthusiasm, it's not really following the rules to ask me for any kind of confirmation. Not that you'll ever get me telling anyone off for not playing by the rules." His pointed glare had Isaac pouting, but they changed the subject.

As she got ready for bed, Jen reviewed the past few hours. Isaac's request to keep it a secret for now raised a few flags, and her inkling of suspicion ramped up when he insisted on monitoring her blood pressure and temperature. Was this why he was doing so-called baseline tests on everyone? After the hints he'd given about experimenting, did it mean someone else had time-travelled? But why all the secrecy? Cogs in her brain did so much more than twirl, but she kept schtum until she could gather more data.

Ch 14 – Murder Most Vile

Cursed Castle

The following session, by mutual request, had everyone meeting in the library for a catch up. As Evadne was still out of play, Jen sat quietly, watching the others interact.

"I say we're being treated like mushrooms." The professor was uncharacteristically strident, gratified by the blank faces. "Kept in the dark and fed bullshit."

Rosalina giggled. "Hear, hear. I don't understand why we're being put in danger with no warning of what we may meet. What harm would it do to give us a heads-up?"

The jester bristled. "You're suggesting we have some control over these sprites. They're a law unto themselves. And let's not underestimate the part you have played in escalating things." A sly glance.

"So you're blaming us?" Grenville protested. "But–"

"If the cap fits." The jester gave a dark sneer.

Kurt took on the role of mediator. "I can see both sides of this spat. The castle management are reluctant to admit to any danger which may result in a lawsuit, but the ghost hunters need warning of life-threatening situations."

Grenville and Rosalina exchanged a glance which said they'd noticed how he'd distanced himself from the team.

The jester scoffed. "All I hear are petty niggles. You're ghost-hunters – surely danger is in the job description."

Rosalina sighed. "This is getting us nowhere. In the light of new information, we'd like to examine the Watergate Tower."

"But that's not next on my schedule. I don't think you

lot appreciate how much trouble I go to in preparing these wonderful expeditions." A petulant pout. "I have one job, and you're not letting me do it properly."

Grenville tried to appease. "We're sorry, and we do appreciate your efforts, truly." He glanced at the others, who nodded agreement. "But we have good reason to believe the Time Tower, as it's been reimagined, or its ghosts, will have a clue to Evadne's whereabouts."

After much grumbling – and a whispered conversation on the walkie-talkie – he complied with their request.

On reaching the study, Kurt set up the equipment, with help from the other two.

Obviously still offended, the jester folded his arms. "This is most irregular. I don't have the full details, but Fulke Greville, aka Baron Brooke, was popular with Elizabeth the First. The traumatic end to Fulke's life has left his restless spirit roaming the halls of his castle home."

A beeping on the meter led Kurt to the portrait and, as they stood beneath it, a dark apparition emerged, taking shape as a white-haired old man.

"Help me, please." The pitiful creature's arms implored.

"What's the problem?" Kurt side-stepped his grasp.

"I never meant to do any wrong. I didn't mean any insult by it; I thought he'd be pleased."

"What are you wittering on about? Insult who and how? Stop talking in riddles and give us facts."

Rosalina tugged him out of the way. "Sorry, sir. You'll have to excuse Kurt, he's worried about our friend. You're Fulke Greville, aren't you?"

"Why yes. But I'm afraid I don't know you, dear lady."

"I'm Rosalina, and we're looking for a tall lady with golden hair – we think she may be here in the tower."

"No ladies in the tower – unless Daisy pops in, which she often does. Quite a beauty, but she has dark hair."

"We've met her. How can we help?"

"I've lost my friend, Sidney. I seem to have been looking forever and a day."

Before he could add more, a tall man in a morning suit burst into the room. "I've just seen that damn fool of a lawyer and he tells me you've made a new will."

"Ralph. Calm down. It's not new. I simply added a codicil giving small bequests to my dependants." His sigh held a strange weariness. "I'd hoped to leave you a lovely little cottage in Mill Street, but something tells me it's not going to satisfy you."

"What would I want with one of those hovels?" Ralph spat his contempt. "I've been true and faithful, given you the best years of my life."

The man ranted about the many ways he'd served the Baron, oblivious to everything but his outrage, and the hunters stood back. Having watched the videos in the Time Tower, they recognised the angry man as Ralph Haywood, but couldn't understand why the frail old man seemed neither angry nor afraid at the violent accusations. If anything, he was more intent on ogling Rosalina.

The tirade over, Haywood folded his long arms. "The least you could give me is the house in Holborn – I deserve to live in London."

"Believe me, I would if I could, just to stop this nonsense, but I can't. It's part of the estate–"

"Liar. If you wanted to, you'd find a way." Haywood unfolded his arms, revealing a knife hidden in the sleeve.

Instead of flinching in horror, Greville opened his rich jacket as though to present a better target to his assailant, seeming to welcome the vicious stabs before melting gracefully to the floor. With a scream, Haywood turned the knife on himself, his wounds fatal.

As Fulke lay on the ground, he beckoned Rosalina over. "Dear lady. Please do something. Some evil darkness is forcing me to relive this scene night after night, and no matter what I do or say it has the same horrific ending."

She nodded. "I want to help. What can I do?"

"I would not ask it of someone so tender, but maybe your rude friend might have the stomach. My physicians will fill my wounds with pig fat instead of disinfecting them. This will turn rancid and infect the wounds, so I will writhe in agony for weeks before blessed death claims me."

"You want him to …?" She mimed slitting her throat.

"I do."

When she explained his request, both men cringed with distaste. Grenville scanned the walls. "I will do it if I have to, but I have no sword."

"That's easily fixed. You may borrow mine." A deep voice startled them all.

"Sir Guy of Warwick. Where did you spring from?"

"I come at this time every eve to put this poor gentleman out of his misery. Whatever evil holds the castle in its thrall is causing misery for all of the spirits." He offered his sword and Grenville stared, his Adam's apple bobbing up and down.

"I'll wager you would prefer me to do the dirty deed."

The professor's head bobbed up and down.

"So be it." He raised his sword and everyone looked away.

"Thank you." Rosalina batted her eyelashes at the heroic figure and he bowed low, kissing her hand.

"Please call on me if you should need rid of a monstrous beast or rescuing from a tower–"

"We'll be sure to do so." Kurt pulled the girl away, dismissing the knight with a wave of his hand.

"Wait." Grenville blocked his path. "Why do you mention rescuing from a tower?"

He deadpanned. "It's a castle with a lot of towers and a long history of locking people up in them."

"Oohhh, get you, Sir Snarky." The jester sniggered.

"But you're not aware of a blonde-haired lady being held in any of them?"

His gaze travelled inward for a moment. "No, I cannot say I am. But do be aware of the secret passages and hidden rooms in many of the buildings."

"Is there one in this tower?" Rosalina asked eagerly.

He frowned. "If there is, I've not seen it."

"Thank you for your help."

"Such as it was." With a curt bow, he left.

As they climbed the stairs to the next level, the jester tried to claw back some of his authority by setting the scene. "You may well meet another Guy – de Beauchamp, from the fourteenth century, by all accounts nothing like his namesake. Quite the political animal, he had a huge grudge against a French commoner, Piers Gaveston, who'd ensnared the Prince of Wales, bleeding him dry."

Kurt glanced up from his meter with a snigger. "Those royals could rarely keep it in their pants."

Several facial muscles around the room reacted to this comment – not because of the sentiment, but the person delivering the line.

The jester's beetled brows won the prize for busiest eye action. He cleared his throat. "His arrogance enraged the established nobility when his military superiority gave him resounding success at the king's tournament in his honour."

"So, low-born but beautiful pisses off toffs. Sounds like a bit of a Cinderella story." Kurt chortled at his own wit.

The giggle-fit transferred like a hungry virus till they were helpless with laughter. "For goodness' sake. *How* old are you?" The jester's sulking cracked them up even more.

The narrator clicked a link and the sound of a door bursting open sobered the ghost hunters. Chains clanked as a prisoner was shoved in and shackled to a chair.

A strident voice led the interrogation. "Piers Gaveston, you are charged with stealing the royal treasure, how do you plead?"

Amusement trilled the reply. "Why would I answer the Black Cur of Arden? You may be the Earl of Warwick, but you have no jurisdiction over me."

The sound of a vicious slap had Rosalina flinching, and the short recording was cleverly done, ending with a dire pronouncement. "I, Guy de Beauchamp, 10th Earl of Warwick, declare that Piers Gaveston has been lawfully tried for treason and sentenced to death. He will be executed on the ninth day of June in the year of our Lord thirteen thousand and twelve."

As darkly dramatic music ended the recording, the door burst open and a man dashed in brandishing a sword. "Where is that blackguard, Guy?"

Stepping in front of Rosalina, Kurt sneered. "If you mean Guy of Warwick, you just missed him."

"Some would name him so. Is that a Welsh accent?"

"Certainly not. I am proud to be German."

"Good for you." He stepped closer. "I was murdered by two Welshmen who took me to nearby Blacklow Hill. One ran me through with a sword, the other beheaded me."

Rosalina squeaked as he grabbed Kurt in an arm lock and pushed his sword tip into the German's side.

"Tell me where he is or I'll run this one through." He peered at Rosalina. "I hear his princess has been locked up in this tower, is that you?"

She shook her head. "As you can see, I am free."

"And you do not have flaxen locks. I *will* find him. Or she will die." Throwing Kurt on the floor he dashed out.

Grenville offered him a hand. "Did you hear that? Flaxen means blonde. It could be Evadne."

"What are we waiting for?" Kurt ran for the door, but Rosalina was closer and she tore up the stairs, dashing into the top room to be met by a dreadful scene.

The angry Frenchman had opened a door to a hidden room, dragging out a chair. Bound to it with thick ropes, Evadne bucked and twisted as he ripped off the tape covering her mouth.

He taunted. "Where is your brave Guy now?"

Rosalina barrelled at him from behind, barely managing

to budge him, and he barked a laugh as his vicious backhand knocked her to the ground.

"Typical of that coward to send wenches to do his work." With the tip of his sword at Evadne's throat, he snarled at her. "Shout for your precious Guy and see if he cares enough to come for you."

Kurt ran into the room, stopping as the sword's tip whipped around, catching his jacket. He stepped back just as Grenville came in, puffing and panting, pushing him back toward the blade.

"Stay back, both of you, or the wenches die." In a flash, he pulled Rosalina up and pushed her so she sat atop Evadne. "Both of you, start screaming and he will appear."

They needed no further prompting as he swung the heavy blade, stopping it dead with the razor sharp edge pressing into their necks.

As the girls screamed the hero's name, Grenville glared angrily but Kurt recovered his senses, asking the narrator whether any weapons were mounted nearby. Before he could answer, Guy of Warwick dashed in, sword at the ready. "Hie villain. Let them go."

"Who are you?" Gaveston frowned.

"He's Guy of Warwick, from medieval times. Looks like you got the wrong Guy." Rosalina couldn't resist.

But nobody chuckled as Gaveston's sword pressed harder, drawing blood. "It's a trick. Guy of Warwick and Guy de Beauchamp, Earl of Warwick are one and the same. You will die – but only after I've killed these people you care about so much."

"Stop." Grenville's knowledge of history finally had its

use. "Guy de Beauchamp, who had you murdered, is not this man. Surely you can see they don't even look alike."

He grunted, glaring.

Grenville tried a different tack. "Piers Gaveston is no coward, threatening helpless women and unarmed men. You're a man of honour with many bold battle victories."

The man's sword-arm trembled, lessening the pressure.

The professor softened his tone. "Was it not your courage and gallantry which impressed King Edward so much he appointed you as weapons master for his son?"

He nodded.

"So would it not be more fitting for you to face the man you think is your enemy in single combat to avenge your death?"

As Gaveston considered this, Guy cleared his throat. "I'm sorry, but that is not possible. My code of chivalry would not permit me raise arms against this poor man after the injustice served to him by my namesake. It would not be honourable." He held out his sword. "However, he deserves justice, so one of you must fight him."

The players glanced at each other before Grenville stepped forward to grasp the sword.

As he stepped back, Guy dealt the most cutting blow. "I must warn you, because of the manner of his death, Gaveston cannot be defeated by being run through with a sword, nor by decapitation. Good luck."

Grenville grasped the long hilt with both hands, slashing the heavy blade through the air as he tried to get the measure of it. Although he'd fenced in university, he knew the carefully-controlled, health-and-safety conscious experience would not serve him well against a skilled swordsman. Steel rang on steel as Gaveston thrust his blade with such dexterity Grenville barely managed to parry before it came at him from a different direction.

Kurt watched with growing concern, shouting advice and warnings, trying to run interference by throwing things to impede Gaveston's success.

Rosalina slipped off the seat, making her way around the room slowly enough to be almost invisible. When she crouched in front of the diamond leaded window pane, she signalled her intention, and Kurt nodded acknowledgement.

As his team-mate faltered, exhausted by the weight of the massive weapon, the German watched for his chance. It came as Grenville stumbled and fell sideways, the sword flying out of his hand. With hitherto unheard-of ability, Kurt grabbed the hilt and ran at their adversary, uttering an ululating war-cry worthy of a great warrior.

Thoroughly flummoxed by the bold attack, Gaveston staggered backwards, falling over Rosalina and toppling backwards with such force the small glass panes could not resist and broke apart, guiding him to his death in the courtyard below.

The silence was only broken by Evadne's snuffles as she wept in the aftermath of trauma.

The narrator called a break, saying to reconvene in ten.

When they returned, Kurt ministered to his stricken partner with a large white hanky and a glass of water.

Rosalina, meanwhile, sat on another chair and, as the strains of her theme tune played on the Wurlitzer, Daisy came through, anger replacing her earlier aloof demeanour.

159

"There you are. I've searched high and low, wondering what on earth could be more pressing than ridding the castle of the foul entity. While the frequency and ferocity of the attacks around the castle have increased, you've been too busy playacting to complete the original task."

Grenville stiffened. "I assure you, dear lady, we've been subjected to our own ferocious attacks. Poor Evadne was captured and we've only just got her back."

"I'm sorry, but you were warned." She glared at them.

Evadne spoke for the first time, turning the spotlight on Daisy. "You claim to be a friend to these poor souls, but your dark deeds have hurt many who might seek revenge."

"I have no idea to whom you refer." She glanced at her former champion, but Grenville shrugged his displeasure and Kurt glanced away, his face stony as his partner grilled.

"People such as Lady Beresford. Is it not true her husband is the true father of Marjorie and Charles?"

The girl gasped, raising a hand to her mouth. "Poor Charlie never even saw his second birthday."

Evadne leaned forward. "Never mind him, what sort of woman asks the Prince of Wales to threaten her lover's standing in society, because his wife got pregnant?"

Her hands flew to her cheeks.

"But *you* came out of it all right, didn't you?" A sneer. "The Prince's 'special favourite' for nearly a decade, with all the trappings of a royal mistress. But it wasn't enough for your voracious appetite, was it?"

Rosalina coughed weakly, but no one moved to help and she reached a trembling hand for the water glass.

As Evadne continued her relentless attack, Grenville

noticed her hair was a darker blonde than he remembered, and her voice became harsh as she probed deeper. "The prince dumped you when he found out your liaison with Joseph Laycock resulted in a fourth pregnancy."

She shook her head sadly. "Stop, please. You make me sound like a horrible person when I was only doing what was expected of aristocrats of my set."

Evadne played her ace. "But someone finally took you to task. Did Robert Blatchford's lengthy article stem from some deep-seated hatred? Had your thoughtless behaviour destroyed someone *he* cared for?"

Rosalina's head jerked up. "Why do you say that?"

A hard stare. "You tell me." Evadne's hair was now completely dark and Grenville nudged Kurt, gesturing at the darkness which surrounded her.

Rosalina's eyebrows tightened. "I cannot think of anything. I approached him to find out more about the lives of the poor." Her outstretched arms implored.

Evadne's voice turned ugly. "Did you honestly think you could blackmail King George into handing over money for his father's love letters to you? And then threaten to sell them to the Americans? How *could* you?"

As Evadne continued to destroy the beleaguered socialite, Grenville took Kurt aside, whispering. "She's obviously under the influence of the big bad, after spending so much time in the tower."

Finally Daisy fled, having had enough, and Grenville wondered aloud how to free a person from evil.

"Only the power of love can free a person from the forces of evil." Rosalina spoke her truth.

Incapable of movement, Grenville seemed in the vice of a binding spell. Kurt had no such impediment as he strode up to his once-beautiful partner, and pulled her out of the chair and the dark miasma surrounding her. Bending his head, he kissed her on the lips.

At first, she responded. Then slowly, as though returning from a nightmare, Jen surfaced, her eyes widening as she realised who was kissing her and struggled to free herself. "No. What?" Shoving him away, she fled the room in tears.

With a hostile glare at her cousin, Georgie ran after her friend.

Ch 15 – Jenny from the Block

June 22

Georgie tapped on Jen's door, waiting for a count of five before knocking again. "Jen? Can I come in?"

Still no answer.

She tried the handle and the door sprang open, but the room was obviously empty. Cringing at the privacy invasion, she repeated the procedure on the bathroom door.

Just as empty.

The noise level on the ground floor heralded the emergence of the boys from the games room. They went into the kitchen, and a moment later, Ben climbed the stairs far enough to spot her leaving Jen's room.

"Is she okay?" He mouthed the words.

"She's not in there." Georgie knelt down so they could talk quietly.

"I'll assume you checked the en-suite. She's not in the kitchen, so unless she went on one of her runs …"

"She wouldn't have had time to change into trainers."

"There's another possibility." He scanned around. "Sometimes, if she wants to get away from it all, she nips into the green bedroom."

Georgie's eyes shot to the two guest rooms at the end of the landing, returning with a frown. "I never knew."

"I'm pretty sure *I'm* not supposed to, but my room is right next door and even the slightest sound travels."

"I don't like to disturb her."

"Normally, I'd agree. But what went on in there wasn't normal." He murmured. "At least I hope it wasn't."

As she pulled up onto her knees, he reached through the railings to touch her arm, his voice low.

"Let me know how she is. I have a bad feeling …"

"Will do." She crept along the corridor, grateful for the noise-cancelling carpet and creak-free floorboards. Outside the room she paused, listening for a sound before tapping the door and opening it gently.

Jen sat on the sheepskin rug, arms circling bent knees in classic foetal position. Rocking back and forth, she shook her head, muttering something Georgie couldn't hear.

Moving slowly, Georgie crossed the room and settled on the floor next to her, unwilling to break whatever trance she was in, or startle her with a touch or word. As she hoped, her presence filtered into Jen's consciousness, which returned to the room with a wan smile.

"Oh, Georgie. What a week."

"And what a way to end it."

Her head tilted, eyes narrowing. "You mean getting rescued from the tower. It was fun – talk about teamwork. I bet Kev had no idea it would go so well when he set it up. Oh, and I loved your line about the wrong Guy. Classic."

Even as she shared the grin, Georgie sensed a difference in her friend: a little too brittle, as though facing up to the following scene where things – especially Evadne – got nasty would disrupt her fragile grip on reality. "Is – er – everything all right?"

More tilting and narrowing. "Of course it is. Why wouldn't it be? I've just spent days at Wimbledon with my gran – what's not to love?"

"With your gran?" Her turn to tilt head and narrow eyes.

164

"You mean you stayed in her old house? That must have been bittersweet, the first time after …" *She died? Way to go on the tactfulness stakes.* Georgie's inner critic scolded.

Thankfully, Jen didn't notice. "Yeah. Vickie was brilliant. She reached the semi-finals of the junior level at only fifteen and the final the next two years."

"Pretty cool." *Since when did she start calling her gran Vickie?* "And then she did the women's competition."

"Sort of. I discovered she qualified for the seniors three years running, from nineteen fifty three to five."

"Don't tell me – your cousin discovered a scrapbook with all the photos and stuff."

Jen smiled. "I never realised quite how beautiful she was back then. She had this radiance about her …" She broke off, her face darkening. It's a shame about the osteoporosis. I never realised that's why her mum was in a wheelchair, it got really bad after she fell the first time, and then she broke her hip." A sigh.

"I never realised you'd met her. You often talk about your gran – I guess it's where the tennis bug started."

She nodded. "I was only seven when Dora died – Mum reckoned I was far too young to go to the funeral, so I had to go to school. I guess she had enough to cope with – Timmy was barely out of nappies, but *he* got to go."

Georgie sensed something drove this uncharacteristic journey into the past. Apart from her gran, Jen rarely mentioned much before high school, as though her life before then was firmly under lock and key. She'd often wondered what trauma could have caused this, but figured Jen would open up when she was good and ready.

"I bet he was a cute baby." Timmy was always a safe bet – Jen adored him.

"The cutest. Gran called him a little ray of sunshine."

"I'm not surprised with you and Tracy doting on him"

A grin. "Mum always said he was her reward for having to put up with three years of me."

"Ouch. That must've hurt."

"Not as much as the colic. Apparently I cried every day for weeks and it drove Dad mental. Despite the midwife's best suggestions about food elimination, nothing worked; not even giving up caffeine. It was basically the start of the rot – Dad threatened to leave her if she didn't shut me up."

"Sounds like the sort of husband women dream of."

A shrug. "I wouldn't know. I barely saw the man apart from when he told me off for doing something which spoilt his 'peace and quiet.' Which meant almost everything."

"What a git. Men like him should be sterilised instead of ruining people's lives. Culling at birth would work better."

"Blimey, that's a bit strong. I didn't know you'd met so many dicks. But your dad was a decent bloke, yes?"

She scoffed. "I suppose he was okay till Mum died, but he was never hands-on – not when he'd got two strapping lads to play football with, and a baby boy to dote on."

Jen nodded. "And the long-distance building gigs – seems we both lucked out on the male role-model front."

"Except your Timmy turned out to be an honest-to-goodness, card-carrying perfect partner. I hope that wife of his knows how lucky she is."

"Trust me, she does. Every time we meet, Karen thanks me and Mum for making him so supportive and laid back."

"I've never met anyone so genuinely interested in people." A grin. "But he's got your irreverent wit."

"I can't take any credit for that. I was always in danger of taking myself way too seriously, but he knew exactly when to blow a raspberry or hug till he squeezed all the badness out of me." An affectionate smile. "Trouble was, he's single-handedly spoilt me for all men – none of them could live up to his impossibly high standard."

Georgie scoffed. "When you look at what's out there, it's not surprising. By the sounds of it, most of the guys in your office would break out in hives if you so much as spoke to them."

Jen laughed. "You got that right. So many Sheldons, momma's boys and – well, Kev. But he's a bit special."

Yep, 'Special' is about right." She air quoted.

"Aww. I didn't actually mean it like that. He's nothing like as bad as he makes out – a bit of a troubled spirit."

Georgie mocked. "You mean wanna-be lady-killer. Sounds like you have a soft spot for him."

"I wouldn't go that far. But in an ideal world there may well be a genuinely caring soul under all the bravado."

"I'll believe that when I see it. But my impression is, away from smart geeky men, most of the rest are closer to your dad's selfish git end of the spectrum."

"Harsh but true." Jen winced. "I'm telling you, Timmy had a narrow escape. He wasn't even a year old when some blonde bimbo stuck her claws in and dragged Dad away. Mum was lecturing at the uni and had to rely on friends to cover when the crèche was closed."

"She did some smart science-y stuff, am I right?"

167

"Microbiology – and she would have been a professor if he hadn't trashed her life."

"Poor Tracy. Some men are total bastards."

"You don't know the half of it. Vickie lived too far away, so his parents stepped in, but they just wanted to declare Mum an unfit mother. She really had to toughen up – just like Dora when her husband died in the war."

"Your great gran?"

"Yep. Anyway, Dad and his new girlfriend tried to take Timmy, and Mum had to fight to keep him. Thankfully one of her colleagues was married to a top barrister and she found enough evidence of his neglect to quash it."

"Thank God. Imagine what he'd have turned out like." Georgie shook her head.

"Doesn't bear thinking about." A shudder.

"But your dad didn't want you?" As soon as the words were out, Georgie wanted to retract them.

Jen scoffed. "As if. He wasn't interested – reckoned I was too bright, like Mum."

"Bullet dodged. And it sounds like a bullshit reason – probably saving face because he knew you wouldn't go." She grimaced. "Sounds like Tracy's well shot of him. Didn't you tell me she's in Australia now?"

"Yep. Her fellah owns a couple of sheep ranches and she's in her element and all loved up to boot. Finally she's found someone to romance her properly.

"He sounds like a real sweetheart."

She shot her a sideways glance. "Reminds me of Ben in a lot of ways. Same level of calm competence."

Georgie giggled. "I thought you were gonna say tall,

dark and handsome."

"Would we say handsome?" She considered. "Maybe not rock-singer or leading-man gorgeous, but a solid lead guitarist or loyal sidekick."

Georgie returned the sidelong glance. "So you've thought about it, then?"

"Don't tell me *you* haven't." Her lips pursed.

"Nope, can't do that."

Jen pounced. "I knew it. You two have been so damned coy every time Kev or Isaac tease it's been a tricky one to call. But I reckon–"

"Whoa, Slow down. We've never – I mean he hasn't–"

"What? Proposed? For goodness' sake girl, when he does, don't keep him hanging. Snap him up as fast as you can, he's one of the good guys."

"Like Timmy?" A sneaky peek.

"Closest I've ever come to matching him."

"I knew it." Georgie wagged a finger. "Why the heck haven't you given the poor guy some encouragement? He's had a thing for you from the first time I met him."

"Ben? No. Surely not."

"Surely has."

A shrug. "He certainly never gave a clue." She frowned. "Wait. When I broke up with Val he was seeing Linda."

"That ended years ago."

"And he's been pining for me ever since? I think not. Anyway, it's too late now. That ship has sailed."

Georgie took all of three nanoseconds. "You met someone down there?"

A beat. "I certainly did. A proper cutie."

169

Georgie didn't know whether to be excited for her friend or disappointed for her other friend. In her head they made a great couple, but it seemed she was the only one who knew how well they were suited. She mustered up a smile. "So, are you going to tell me all about him?"

With an enigmatic glance – somewhere between coy and "mind your own beeswax" – she chuckled. "Soon."

Jen went to bed shortly after dinner, pleading exhaustion, and Isaac seemed most concerned, asking if she needed her migraine medication.

"No, I don't have the warning signs, but unless I get a good night's sleep, it's a given."

"Trouble sleeping?" Kev looked up. "You know the best cure for that."

She rolled her eyes. "Apart from sex?"

He pouted. "I wasn't actually thinking that, but if you're interested …" A leer.

Another roll. "Go on then. What were you thinking?"

"I've no idea now – all I have is this image–"

"Stop right there."

"*I gotta know right now. Before we go any further, do you love me?*" Ben and Georgie chorused the Meatloaf lyrics in harmony, high-fived, and fizzled out at Jen's glare.

Kev chuckled. "I *could* give you an answer in the morning, but I fear it will be too late."

"Let me sleep on it." Jen flounced out, head held high, and then turned back with a cheeky grin. "Gotcha! Go on then. What's this non-sex-based cure for sleeplessness?"

"Mum reckons it always worked for her. You tense

every muscle in the body, then relax it, starting from feet up to head and then back down again."

She nodded. "I've tried it."

"Then you go over every aspect of your day from breakfast, recalling any incidents. Don't dwell: if it went pear-shaped, look for the lesson, or if it was good, give thanks. Then move on; it's a mind-clearing thing."

"And?"

"That's it. I've tried it a couple of times – I rarely got past lunch before zoning out completely."

"Thanks. I'll try it." As she left, Isaac followed her out, suggesting he took her vitals because they might indicate a variation from her normal readings.

Georgie couldn't resist heckling Kev. "Since when did you do woo-woo?"

Without deigning to answer, he disappeared, presumably on a DM-related task, leaving Ben and Georgie on the sofa again.

"Well? How is she?" Ben's lack of preamble hinted at his concern, reinforcing her view that he still cared for Jen.

"Honestly?" A head shake. "Not quite the full shilling."

"I *knew* it. Sometimes it's hard to separate a person from the characters their playing in a session, but the way she attacked poor Daisy felt like more than an act. It was as though she had a genuine grievance against her – or someone. I've no idea where she got all the stuff from."

"That's easy. Apparently her gran was a huge fan and had a copy of the book Daisy wrote. So Jen read it when she was in Wimbledon. And that's another thing. When she spoke about her gran it was like she'd actually met her."

"Sorry, what? She knew her for over three decades."

"But not as a beautiful young woman."

He tapped a nail on his teeth. "It's the first time she's been down there since her gran died. She'll have been poring through her gran's tennis scrapbook."

"But photos wouldn't show the radiance Jen talked about." A beat. "And it was so odd – she called her Vickie and referred to Dora instead of gran and great-gran. I've never known her do that before."

His eyes narrowed. "That *is* out of character. I can't think of a good reason. Apart from the obvious."

She frowned. "You mean time travel?" A scoff.

"Yeah, you're right, we could be a little on the obsessed side over that. And I'm sure she'd have said something."

"Like we did, you mean."

"True." His turn to scoff. "Anything else?"

Georgie glanced away, reluctant to divulge anything.

"What? Come on, mate. If there's something bad going on, we need to figure it out and help her through it. That's what friends do."

"I don't think it's anything bad exactly."

"Something good then. Her cousin's pregnant again? Timmy's wife has whelped? OMG – *Jen's* not pregnant is she? Not sure if that would be good or bad."

"What makes you think of babies? Getting broody?"

"Well if it's not babies or puppies – a bloke? *Computer says yes*. Did she meet someone? What's he like?"

Cursing her lack of poker-face, Georgie shrugged. "She refused to talk about it. At all."

Ch 16 – Wicked Witch

The jester glared around the library as though daring one of the team to say something. When no one did, he grunted. "Well I hope you're all satisfied with yourselves. I warned you what might happen if you didn't follow the rules, and the worst happened."

His hostile gaze rested on Evadne. "I trust you're recovered from your ordeal."

No muscle on her face revealed her desperate need to clarify which ordeal – the kidnap, possession or kiss.

"Seeing as how you've decided you know better than I about where to investigate–"

As ever, Grenville pulled on his peacemaker pants. "Please accept our humble apologies. We meant no offence, but we were all consumed by the need to rescue our companion, and it seems we got to her just in time."

"Really? Just in time to stop her from being infiltrated by the hostile entity? I think not." He glared at her. "And are you completely convinced she's free of his influence now? If it were up to me, I'd suspect every word coming out of her mouth."

Rosalina protested. "That's because you don't know her as we do. Evadne may come across as a tad on the acerbic side, but–"

"Me? Acerbic? How dare you, you glorified pikey?" The shrill abuse and toxic glare had them all cringing back, swapping anxious glances. Then she exploded into girlish laughter with a wink. "Sorry, but you should see your faces. Lighten up, guys. Surely you know all that rudeness is an act for the cameras?"

"Er, no, actually." Kurt's expression wobbled, hinting at some dark hurt.

She nudged him. "Of course you do."

He flinched from her touch, but she didn't notice, carrying on. "I tell you often enough how I couldn't do any of this without you."

"Sometimes I think you'd prefer my predecessor."

The jester perked up. "I heard he was a right prick."

She glanced quizzically. "You might think so from his reputation. He actually showed great promise, but he was unlucky; the money men wanted something different. Just like they insist the viewers love a rude British woman – look how the Yanks took Anne Robinson to their hearts. *You* are the weakest link, goodbye." A smirk.

The jester cleared his throat. "This is a little more serious than your average bump in the night."

Kurt's sour tone matched his expression. "Then we shouldn't waste time with this nonsense. Where are we on the riddle?"

Grenville exchanged a glance with Rosalina at the palpable atmosphere, and he coughed. "For the second letter, I worked on 'not steady' anagrams and I came up with some interesting things. 'Stay noted,' 'Not y dates,' and 'don't say et.' Then I remembered we need a name and got Tony Stade, Stan Toyed and Dean Tosty."

Kurt scoffed. "Because those are likely."

"Then I remembered Je – Evadne saying she'd used a synonym. Constant is synonym for steady 'like days of old,' which gives the anagram 'consonant TT.' And Evadne said she had the letters TT left over. So the second letter is a consonant."

As people congratulated his deductive powers, Rosalina spoke up. "My gran used to have a rhyme whenever she saw a magpie– one for sorrow, two for joy–"

"Three for a girl and four for a boy." Grenville grinned.

"Five for something, six for gold." Rosalina continued.

"Silver." Evadne put in.

"No, it's definitely gold, because it rhymes with a story never to be told." Rosalina flicked an annoyed glance. "As in the first clue."

"Seven for a story never to be told." Grenville finished the rhyme. "So the answer's seven? But we need a letter."

"Maybe it's a substitution code." Kurt smirked. "You know, where numbers stand for letters."

"The seventh letter's G." Rosalina squealed. "OMG. Guy, it must be."

"The Y sits next to X, which is double V." Kurt's observation came an instant before Grenville's protest.

"But the U is a vowel, not a consonant."

"Almost there." Evadne winked, happy to be back in the game and running rings around the intellectuals.

"How do you mean?"

"The clue is *not constant*, so *not* a consonant."

Greville groaned. "No way – that's cheating."

"What else do you expect from a trickster?" She glanced at the jester, who made an elaborate bow.

Kurt pouted. "I don't see where you got constant from, steady has dozens of synonyms, and that one doesn't suggest 'days of old' to me."

Evadne chuckled – this was a big win. "I – er – reverse engineered it." Her eyes twinkled as she emulated his pomposity. "Given the preponderance of consonants for the third letter, it seemed likely the second would be a vowel."

"Enough." Kurt sniffed. "Given it's Guy, which one?"

"My money's on the nasty piece of work who had the angry French man horribly murdered." Evadne offered.

"I can't see it being the Dragon-slayer – he's way too heroic." Rosalina added.

"Hang on." Grenville put the brakes on. "Now we know the middle letter's a vowel and the last one is one of a, c, d, f, l, n, v, w, x and y, we should look at all the permutations before deciding it has to be Guy."

By the time they'd all had a play, their lists all had dozens of crossed out possibilities.

Rosalina read through Kurt's, spotting Ben, Jen and Kev. She frowned. "Why aren't these crossed out? We haven't met anyone with these names."

"Do you know that for sure? Any number of folks could be called one of these names."

"In that case, here's another one." She wrote down Zac.

His eyes flared before he controlled it. "I suppose it is sufficiently biblical – could have been one of the roundhead guards."

Evadne collected up all the possible names, making a new list. Everyone had Mol, Dan the stable boy and Guy. Kurt included Pol and Grenville had Gaveston.

"But that has more than three letters." Kurt sneered.

"The riddle doesn't specify how many letters, it merely

says 'the whole will surprise – you thought you knew better.' Which tends me toward Polly and good Guy."

"Who can we rule out?"

"Tom, surprisingly – except, that wouldn't surprise me at all." Rosalina giggled.

"Well in that case we can rule out everyone else in this room." Kurt sniggered.

"Do we know the name of the gaoler? I would say that has to be top of the list from our most recent research." Evadne saw several nods at her suggestion.

Rosalina shivered. "I always figured it would end up in the dungeons. I guess we'll have to man up and go for it."

"Just a moment. All we have to do is check the Time – sorry, Watergate – Tower tonight. If poor Fulke is still in his groundhog day then we'll know it wasn't Gaveston." Grenville beamed. "When was it?"

"In around half an hour. Long enough for you to procure yourself a sword from the armoury. I would suggest you ladies find yourself a suitable weapon, too. I have the feeling we will meet some dark evil tonight." The jester glanced at Kurt. "Your request to set up equipment in the dungeon has been granted, you should have time to do that if you hurry along."

Rosalina glanced at him. "Need some help?"

"No!" As the jester glared, Kurt shook his head.

"I'll be fine. You should protect yourselves. Is there not a quilted hauberk they can borrow?"

Grenville scoffed. "A hauberk is the chainmail worn over the padded undervest, which could be a gambeson–"

"We'll find something suitable." His oily smile back in

place, the jester waved Kurt on, then led the others up some backstairs to a wardrobe room. It was filled with various costumes worn by the castle's live-action players and reenactors, and he kitted them out with the protective jackets, quipping they were the Kevlar of their day.

"Right. We'll need to shortcut through the kitchens, so keep up, professor." The jester shot out, running down the corridor, and even Rosalina couldn't match his speed, wearing a jacket which was probably as heavy as the armour which would have gone over it. Evadne struggled and a sweat-drenched Grenville didn't have a chance.

When they reached the ground floor, the jester had disappeared. Always mindful of her environment, Rosalina had studied the plans and knew roughly where the kitchens were. As they approached, an ominous clattering behind had them hurrying along.

Evadne risked a peek behind. "It looks like the suits of armour we passed at the foot of the staircase."

"But they were empty – the visors were up and I looked inside." Grenville panted, glancing back. "It is them. Empty or not, they're moving faster than we are."

A door opened on the left and a hand beckoned. "In here, quick." A flash of grey disappeared into the room.

Dashing in, they were delighted to see the rows of gleaming copper pans and two massive fireplaces – they'd found the kitchen, but no sign of the jester. They whirled as the door closed and two sturdy bolts slid into place.

"Shhh. Quiet and they'll pass." Barely a whisper.

Evadne's eyes narrowed as she studied the speaker, spotting yellow stains on her apron, woollen socks above wooden clogs and dark ringlets escaping the frilly hat. Scanning around for further clues, she felt the weight of the girl's gaze as the clattering stopped by the door.

A loud thump made Grenville jump and his head collided with one of the pans which swung toward the next one, hoping to start a cascading peal worthy of the bells calling the faithful to Sunday mass.

Grenville froze and the girls held their breath, but the maid moved like lightning, using his chest as a springboard as she leapt up and caught the edge of the pan, stilling it as the thumping of two heavy gauntlets intensified.

She dropped to the floor, nimble as a cat, but her foot slipped in a shiny patch on the floor and she clung onto him as the door rattled against the sturdy iron bolts. Her eyes darted to one of the bolts which she hadn't turned all the way into the lock position. It moved under the vibrations resulting from the relentless attack. Fearless, she released her hold, her intention clear.

But Grenville caught her shoulders and, in response to the angry stare, put his finger to his lips, pointing. The noise had stopped, replaced by resounding silence.

She slipped from his grip and listened at the door. "They're gone." Her hand crept up to the first bolt.

"Wait." Evadne's whisper gave her pause. "We didn't hear the sound of retreating feet."

"I promise. They're gone. It happens every night at this time." A shrug. "At least it has for a long while."

Grenville nodded. "Which explains why you weren't more frightened. Just like Fulke."

She tilted her head to the side in a familiar move, her

179

expression neutral.

He thrust out a hand. "Sorry. Where are my manners? I'm Peter Grenville. And you are?"

"Martha. Pleased to meet you, your Lordship." She bobbed a curtsy. "Is this your wife? She dresses strangely."

Evadne smothered a grin. "Yes. I'm Lady Grenville. You're a milkmaid, I believe."

Winking, she gestured at the large churn, glistening with yellow butter. "What gave it away?" Her gaze hardened as she peered at Rosalina. "I'm surprised his Lordship allows you people in the castle, let alone his kitchen."

"You people?"

"Wise women, some people call them, but most say witches. Do you deny you deal with herbs and plants?"

"No. But I only use them to heal and help."

"And never to harm?" She spat on the ground. "I don't believe it. Mark my words, you'll get there one day. Once someone takes ill against a woman, there's all manner of things they can do to destroy her."

As she shook her head, Evadne finally twigged. This milkmaid was Moll Bloxham, the witch, and their research had shown her to be a nasty piece of work. *They were in serious trouble.* She mouthed the word "Moll" at the other two, cringing as the girl's features twisted and her tone sharpened. "That weakling Earl believed the stories and said I was caught stealing, sending me to the stocks in the courtyard. Have you any idea how humiliating it is to have people who should know better throwing ripe tomatoes, soggy cabbage and rotten, stinking potatoes at you?"

They glanced uneasily at each other.

"Answer me, damn you." Her face darkened.

"No." They answered in tentative unison.

"Let me show you." With a snap of her fingers, she pointed at a large basket of vegetables, and several potatoes, green with mould, slowly rose into the air.

Evadne's eyes narrowed as she spied Moll's ringlets had straightened, losing their gloss. *Curiouser and curiouser.*

Another snap had the spuds shooting at the team, but they bounced off the padded jackets with barely a thud.

"That's no fun. I was bruised for weeks afterwards." At her twirling hand, a dozen black carrots lined up. A third snap had them targeting vulnerable spots on their faces.

"Close your eyes and–" A large carrot entered Grenville's mouth, cutting off his warning, and he choked, turning his back as he pulled it out.

The girls followed suit, turning away from the missiles, but with a cackle, Moll sent the next volley of rotten vegetables spinning around them, attacking from all directions. "Not very nice, is it? They accused me of short-changing customers, so you three can have all of this in recompense." The bottom few layers had decomposed to a pulp of onions, tomatoes and soft fruit. As these rose, she targeted them high so they smashed against the copper pans, bursting and dripping onto her victim's heads. When they tried to cover their heads with their arms, another snap had their arms down by their sides and the cords on the jackets wrapped themselves around, knotting the ends. As she worked, her youthful beauty drained, blotching her skin and turning her hair to straw.

"They say I unleashed a supernatural campaign of terror

against the town of Warwick itself, but why would I? All my family and friends lived there." Another cackle. "I believe you've met some of my descendants, strapping stable lads, both. See, before they branded me a witch, I, too was a wise woman." She approached Rosalina. "You fancied my Tom, didn't you?" The lack of an immediate answer had her screeching. "DIDN'T YOU?"

Ignoring the theatrics, Rosalina smiled with sadness. "Tom was a character all right. Cheeky, fun and so brave." Her voice choked. "He saved my life. And now he's dead."

"Because of you? I heard he died a hero, saving some nob from an enemy spy."

"He did. Such a hero." She shook her head.

"But a dead one, all the same." Wistfulness replaced her anger, but only for a second. "And for that, you will all die." Another snap saw a tall, carved dresser divest itself of the earthenware plates, dishes and beakers, which hurled themselves across the kitchen at the team. The effort of this magic hastened the aging with her skin wrinkling and hair turning white. Her bony, pointing finger tracked around the kitchen, commanding each station into play, ending with the butcher's block which housed several sharp knives. Another cackle and she fled, leaving behind absolute chaos.

Grenville sprang into action as the ties binding his arms loosened. "Quick, free your arms." Meanwhile, he unhooked six of the largest copper pans, giving them two each to batter away the missiles as they ran for the door, which inexplicably remained bolted from the inside.

Rosalina couldn't get the heavy metal rods to budge – they were crusted with rust. She wailed in frustration.

Grenville's attempt had no more success. "Where's a can of WD40 when you need one?"

Evadne got them to move as she applied butter she'd scooped from the churn and forced it into every crevice, wiggling the bolts to free them. Meanwhile, the other two stood behind, playing the weirdest mixed-doubles tennis match with copper pans and the contents of the kitchen.

"How far are we from the knives?" She was almost crying in frustration at the lack of progress, despite every square inch of skin on her hands being covered in greasy butter, turned red by the rust.

"Another couple of minutes, I'd say."

"You two should look for cover. These things aren't gonna give up any time soon."

"Never gonna happen." Rosalina chuckled. "My backhand's improved no end."

"What it needs is brute force and ignorance. I'd 'hit it wiv an 'ammer' if I had one. Stand back."

As she complied, he swung his thick-bottomed pan at the bolts and they both shifted. Another couple of blows had them loose enough to shift past the edge of the door. He pushed with all his might, but it didn't budge.

"Wait." Rosalina pulled up the metal ring and twisted – a separate latch. They dashed out and, as they closed the door, a hail of thumps said they'd made it just in time as a blade made its way through the gap between the doors.

"Something tells me we've no need to go to the Watergate Tower." Grenville said dryly.

Evadne giggled. "I think we can safely assume Gaveston wasn't the big bad."

"So where now? The dungeon?" Rosalina winced as something trickled down her face, dashing it away.

Raising her greasy hands, Evadne grimaced. "I'm not going anywhere until I've washed this lot away. The kitchen would be the obvious place, but …"

Grenville frowned, pointing to the door – the knife blade had gone. "I think it will be okay now." He turned the iron ring and the heavy door swung open.

"I'm not sure …" Rosalina's reluctance said she'd been more affected by the woman's antics than she let on.

Peeking in, he whistled. "Ladies. You will not believe this." He pushed the door wider and they entered, staring at the spotless kitchen with everything in its place.

"Oh, my gosh. Your hands." Rosalina pointed at Jen's equally spotless hands, then felt her hair, no longer drenched in rotten food.

"Oh-ka-ay. Let's step away from the creepy kitchen, folks." Grenville backed out and they made their way down the corridor, musing. "Interesting that the jester kitted us out with these jackets just in time for that bombardment."

"I know. Almost as if he knew." Evadne deadpanned.

"Equally interesting that a certain German film producer just happened to be called away." Rosalina winked.

They skirted around the empty suits of armour, to find the door to the great hall had been locked.

"We can bypass it if we go up the stairs." Rosalina's attention to the geography of the place really paid off. It meant getting a lot closer to the forbidding guards than any of them were comfortable with, and they all dashed between them as though running a gauntlet.

As they levelled with the wardrobe room, the jester appeared, in an awful tizz. "What happened to you lot? All hell's kicking off upstairs and you've gone AWOL."

"Show us," Evadne commanded. "Where's Kurt?"

"He's up there trying to capture some footage for the show, but Moll has gone crazy, ranting about people who shouldn't be meddling in things they don't understand. What did you do to make her so angry?"

"Exist?" Rosalina snorted. "She was an argument waiting to happen and would have turned her wrath on anyone who walked into the kitchen. Where you were supposed to lead us."

Declining to answer, he led them up a narrow staircase, turning at the top. "This is where she was last seen, so weapons at the ready." The door fetched up on a roof.

"But *that's* Caesar's Tower." Rosalina pointed to where Kurt filmed from his position at the top of the oval tower. They shouted at him to take cover as Moll turned into a huge white wolf and leapt across the ramparts, scrabbling to land on the sub-turret. The wolf placed its front paws on the crenellations and howled – an angry, powerful wail.

This was met by an ear-bleeding screech drawing their eyes upward as a huge red dragon thundered toward the tallest tower, hurling fire at the defenceless Kurt.

The last thing they saw was his burning figure leaping over the battlements.

Ch 17 – The Return of Stepford-Jen

June 2022

The session had gone on until the wee, small hours got all growed up, and they all lay in till nearly midday on the Sunday. The delicious smells of freshly-baked bread, proper percolator coffee and sizzling bacon drew them down to the kitchen where Kev had on a white chef's cap and his retro vinyl apron with a naked woman on the front.

"Good morning – or should I say, afternoon – campers."

Various grunts and groans met his cheery salute, and Ben shaded his eyes. "Can we get a dimmer switch on the brightness, please?"

"I was gonna say volume control." Georgie high-fived.

"Can we make it a mute button?" Jen clutched her ears. "Sorry, mate, I don't mean to sound ungrateful after you've gone to so much trouble, but I barely slept last night."

His knee-jerk reaction of, "None taken," tailed off as he peered at her. "Blimey, Jen. Are you okay? Sit down, pet." He steered her to a seat.

As ever, it passed Isaac by as he grabbed a plate and snatched a croissant. "Mmmm. Thanks for this, Kevin."

"Yeah, thanks, mate, you've played a blinder." Ben added belatedly, and Georgie gave a thumbs up.

Jen felt slightly ashamed because her housemates' concern for her had overshadowed the magnificent efforts Kev had made to feed them. She squeezed his arm as he hovered. "I don't know where you found the energy, but this is a delightful treat, and we really appreciate it."

"Honestly, I never thought I'd say these words, but the

pleasure's all mine. I'm just so grateful for the way you've all borne with me while I get to grips with the phenomenal task of being a DM. I know I've said it before, but hats off to Isaac for doing it so well."

He shrugged it off with a sniff. "Practice makes slightly better. Every campaign teaches you things about yourself and your party."

Ben clapped him on the back. "Very deep, mate, but you're undoubtedly the king of kings. I think Jen and Kev have done well for first timers, and I'm only glad I have a while before doing mine. I've done a ton of research, but I want to learn from everyone else's … ideas."

"You were gonna say mistakes." Kev glared. "Fess up."

"Even after years, you still have no idea what really goes on in my head." Ben deadpanned.

"Whatever, mate – you know I'm right."

"The only man who never makes a mistake is the man–"

"Who never does anything. Theodore Roosevelt, 1900." The others chorused with a plethora of grins.

Isaac sniffed. "I was going to say 'who never tried anything new.' It seemed more apt in this case. And it was attributed, albeit weakly to Albert Einstein, although I believe many others have expressed similar sentiments."

Kev chuckled. "Good old Isaac. We'd soon know if you were ever affected by the big bad because you'd stop talking like the pedantic offspring of a dictionary mating with a thesaurus."

His face put several withered lemons to shame. "And we'd know with you because there would be no mention of coitus in its many forms. Even reference books."

Georgie joined in. "Ben would become rude, arrogant, selfish—"

"And sexy as hell." Kev grinned at her. "And you would be a total slob, wasting resources willy-nilly and oblivious to the power of nature."

Jen felt the weight of all their gazes as each one went through some kind of back-pedal, swapping embarrassed glances. *Curiouser and curiouser.* "I suppose I'll have to say it if you're all so scared of upsetting me. I'd become sweet and gentle, a proper Mary-Sue being nice to everyone and mothering the crap – sorry, bejaysus – out of them. What? I know what a tyrant I can be."

Georgie sent a stricken glance at Ben before shaking her head. "Actually, most of that's who you already are. Nope. If we're going for opposites, you'd be thick as pig-shit, timid and a total klutz in the kitchen."

She chuckled as the others nodded, studiously avoiding her gaze as they went round for second helpings of the divine breakfast. Something niggled in the back of her mind, but she couldn't put her finger on it. "Anyone else get an awful nightmare about Kurt jumping off that tower?"

With a mouthful of food, Georgie raised her fork to agree. Ben shrugged and, from the corner of her eye, she spotted a weird exchange between Kev and Isaac. Dismissing it as her imagination, she continued. "Actually, I've been having recurring mares for a while now. The world is a huge saucer and I'm teetering on the edge. Then a train screams past and I'm falling into an abyss."

Isaac's eyes narrowed and Georgie's flicked toward Ben before she swallowed. "My dreams have been taken over by all the ghosts we've seen in the castle, but they've mostly been benign until the Time Tower. I keep reliving Gaveston's journey from Warwick Castle to that hill." A shudder.

Kev frowned. "But I never included any of that in the scene. I researched it all, but decided against it."

Georgie scoffed. "What can I say? This stuff feels close to home. Like, I've been there before, if that makes sense."

"Not really, but this is you, pet. Who knows what goes on in that woo-woo head of yours?"

Jen rolled her eyes, submitting to Isaac's request to check her vitals with a meek timidity which had the other three chuckling. He suggested they went to the lounge so she could sit quietly for the requisite fifteen minutes, suggesting she could run the meditation app he'd loaded onto her phone to help diminish the effects of a sleepless night. It seemed sensible, although a small part of her wanted to wonder if that wasn't fudging the results, but a distant memory suggested individual glitches were to be expected, only the overall trends mattered.

When he'd finished, he disappeared off for his regular Sunday-afternoon siesta, even though they all knew from the noises coming from his room he wasn't sleeping. He just liked to watch an old black-and-white movie without anyone taking the mick about his old-man repertoire, which usually meant old war movies or classic gumshoe.

Her fuzzy head led her back to the kitchen for the clarity only ibuprofen brought, but she stopped dead as she heard Ben and Georgie's discussion as they cleared up.

"Seriously, I reckon we should say something to her. If

Kev and Isaac *are* doing something dodgy, I'm a hundred percent she's not involved."

"Who'd have thought it? Talk about an unlikely pairing? But then I thought the same about her and Isaac."

"Absolutely. I really struggled when she came out with that 'Mary-Sue' description. It was so close to Stepford-Jen, I swear it was written all over my face."

She'd heard enough, and her conspicuous throat-clearing before entering the kitchen had guilt writ large across their faces. "Stepford-Jen?"

At least they had the decency not to deny it. Georgie led, a strange expression on her face. "We've noticed a difference in you in the past few weeks. Is there anything you want to tell us?"

"About what?"

"Your trip to Wimbledon, for example."

"Nothing much to tell. I went down to watch the championship for the first time in a while and ended up going behind the scenes with Vickie." A grin. "The dinner with Joe and Freddie was pretty cool. What?"

"Vickie, as in your gran – ex-junior champion?"

Jen frowned. "Of course. I don't know many Vickies."

"Who died several years ago."

"Wait, what?" A beat. "But she … Shit." She pressed her hands into her face, hunching up her shoulders.

"Were you in nineteen fifty-five by any chance?"

Memories came tumbling through. Betty's elevenses, Dora's leg in plaster, Vickie's pregnancy worries. "Was it real? Did I really travel back in time?" A head shake.

Drying her hands, Georgie darted over as Jen's legs sent

190

a request to her brain requesting immediate instruction on the whole supporting her body scenario and their part in it.

"Whoa, girl. Sit here. It's a helluva shock."

Ben appeared with a glass of water and an ibuprofen. "Take this, bab. It'll help with that muzzy head."

Georgie's comedic glower had him shrugging, his tone more than a tad defensive. "I notice these things."

"We all know that, but bab?"

"It's what I call my sisters. They seem to like it."

"Yet you call me mate?"

A blush. "I thought you'd find bab patronising."

She scoffed. "Yeah, you're probably right."

"I like it. Dead cute." Jen put the glass down with a snigger. "Like my fiancé."

"Wait, what? When did you get engaged?"

A giggle. "Not for real, just like a D&D character. I had to pretend – wait. I'm not supposed to tell anyone."

Ben spotted her concern and reassured. "It's fine. The DM gave us a level nine clearance."

She puffed out a breath. "Thank goodness. I don't want to cross him; I wouldn't like him when he's angry."

"You know this is all part of your debrief? Probably the most important part of the entire mission." Georgie's tone suggested she was the senior operative, and Ben's admiring glance confirmed it.

Jen saluted. "Sir, yessir."

"At ease, soldier. Just give us your report."

~*~

Ben glanced at Georgie, hoping she'd have the chops to pull this off, but she seemed well-versed in the lingo and protocols as she teased out the story of how Jen had met her gran. How she'd stayed in her house to watch the last few days of the 1955 Wimbledon championship before Isaac appeared to bring her back, posing as her fiancé.

"And you returned straight back to this 2022?"

She frowned. "How do you mean, *this* 2022. Are you implying there's another one?"

Georgie floundered and he stepped in. "It's just a ploy we use to check if you're paying attention."

"Oh right. Mum's the word, eh?" She tried to tap the side of her nose, but her finger missed and she giggled, gesturing with the glass. "I don't know what this is, but it's strong stuff."

He made a show of sniffing the liquid with a grimace, chucking it, and then refilling from the tap.

"Thank you." She gulped it back in one and as she put the glass down, Jen returned with a blink. *"What the what?"* A sigh. "It happened again, didn't it?"

"What did?"

"I dunno for sure. It's like I zone out or something. Bugger." Her hands flew up to her temples.

"Here, let me try." Georgie spread her fingers, encircling Jen's head, and massaged.

She instantly relaxed. "Mmm, feels good."

"Aye, aye, what's all this then?" Kev walked in, reacting as only he could. "Looks like a Vulcan mind meld. Earth to Jen, come in, Jen."

"Bog off, Kev." Georgie glared.

"No can do. Until we've sorted out a time to resume. Of course if you'd prefer to leave Kurt hanging…" A chuckle.

"And if you knew anything about the castle's architecture, you'd know he could be hanging off an actual cliff."

"Sounds fine to me." Ben gestured. "I'm not sure Jen's really up to another session. Pretty sure this is the result of her not sleeping thanks to your nightmare world."

"Pardon me for being such a talented DM." His grin faltered. "Seriously, Jen. I'm sorry if my campaign's done that to you, but I thought you were made of sterner stuff."

Her eyes sprang open and she shot up. "No Vickie, he's not my fiancé. Not for real, just like a D&D character. I had to pretend – wait. I'm not supposed to tell anyone." She hurried off.

"What the fuck?" Kev jumped back. "What have you done to her?"

"Not us, trust me."

"Who then, Isaac?" Kev's sceptical frown said not.

This told Ben what he needed to know. It was too soon to let on. "I couldn't say for sure, we've both noticed Jen's brain glitching, ever since the release."

"She was under a lot of stress – we all were. But now she's had a nice relaxing week of watching tennis, she'll soon be back firing on all cylinders."

"Yeah, I'm sure you're right, mate. About half an hour okay? Give her some time for the pills to work."

Kev frowned. "If you're sure she'll be okay. It may get a tad heavy."

"She'll be fine." *Apart from the leap off a cliff.*

Ch 18 – Grisly Goaler

Cursed Castle

"Noooooooooo!" Evadne's scream pierced the air, attracting the dragon's attention and he glared at them and roared, stunning them into inactivity. With a flick of his tail, he breathed in deeply and, stretching out his wings, launched himself off the tower, flying with grace and beauty which kept them mesmerised.

Unable to move anything but her head, Evadne scanned around to see Rosalina and Grenville similarly afflicted. "Where's the jester?" Her words barely forced themselves past stiffening jaw muscles, but both their gazes were fixed on the creature as it turned slow circles around them, licking its lips, a glow building in its belly as it prepared for the next fiery breath.

She'd been in some pickles in her time, but Kurt had always been beside her, sharing, supporting and generally having her back. But now he was dead – either burnt alive or splattered on one of the many hard surfaces surrounding the tower. The slim chance he could have landed in the moat, gave the tiniest sliver of hope, and she sent a prayer up to whatever gods might be listening that he'd escaped.

Her research had made several references to Guy as Dragon-slayer, so she tried to call him, but no sound came out. Glancing at Rosalina, she noticed her deep frown of concentration and wondered whether the girl's belief in the power of thought might help. Although unable to summon him with her voice, she pictured the brave knight and shouted his name in her mind. *"Please, Sir Guy of*

Warwick, we need your help."

The door burst open, seizing the creature's attention and breaking the spell binding them in place.

"Quickly adventurers – you must go to the dungeon." Guy pulled each of the women to safety with his free hand. "The Frankish man is in dire peril."

Frankish? That meant German – Kurt. Evadne wasted no time, even as she heard Guy assuring Grenville he needed no help with the monster, being old adversaries.

Descending the spiral staircase at speed proved tricky, even keeping close to the wall where the triangular steps were widest. Although many had been replaced with concrete blocks topped with a roughened surface, some of the original stone remained, polished to a glacial surface by the footprints of many millions of visitors. She slowed, recognising the futility of breaking a limb – or her neck – due to reckless haste.

From above, she heard a squeal, thump, and Grenville's very slightly miffed, "Oh bother." He shouted down. "Take care, ladies, some of these steps are treacherous."

Rosalina caught up with her as they reached the ground floor, taking the lead as they hustled through to Caesar's Tower, where poor Kurt had – no. Evadne shook away the thought, determined to visualise him as whole and alive.

Approaching the dungeon, their delicate noses were assaulted by a stench which combined damp, decay and a metallic note which could only be blood. They slowed as Grenville limped along, puffing, panting and holding his nose. He chortled. "Oh, for a nosegay."

But they were in no mood for an explanation as their

195

ears were assailed by inhuman growls and the screams of anguished souls being tortured, amid the pitiful pleas of prisoners to be set free. Dim lights, barely enough to see a yard ahead, flickered a few times then went out, plunging the narrow tunnel into darkness. The thump of heavy footsteps had them squeezing to one side and Grenville's shoulder was shoved so violently he stumbled, just as the lights came back on. He saw no one; however a putrid, sweaty smell had them choking anew.

"Remind me what we know?" Since her capture, Evadne's ability to retain facts had all but evaporated.

Grenville needed no notes. "A truly malevolent spirit, believed to be a sadistic gaoler who delighted in torturing the prisoners in his charge. He's been known to assault people by shoving and scratching them. Well, I can vouch for the shoving." He held his shoulder.

"I read something about poltergeist activity." Rosalina piped up. "Or was that Moll?"

"She could certainly whip up a storm in a teacup." Evadne chuckled. "Or should that be a beaker?"

"And something about him glaring from behind a metal grate and yelling at people. I really don't fancy channelling him – they say his eyes glow like hot coals."

The tunnel opened out into a room where an ominous metal contraption hung from the ceiling, a body slumped inside. A fire burnt in the corner and the tips of several torture instruments glowed red. The large, sweaty man poking the fire, turned, poker in hand. "Who're you lot? No one's supposed to come down here when I'm working."

Evadne went for humble charm. "We're so sorry to

disturb you, good sir. We're looking for my fia– betrothed. Sir Guy mentioned he might be down here."

"Do-gooding bastard thinks he can order me about–"

"I cannot imagine anyone ordering *you* about." Rosalina took a step closer, swinging her hips to draw his eye. "You have the likeness of a man skilled at his trade."

"That I am, lass. What's a pretty young thing like you doing down here? 'Tis no place for such a fine piece."

She bobbed a curtsy. "Thank you for your kindness. But my poor sister is beside herself with worry and we've searched everywhere else."

Sounds echoed down the corridor: a childish giggle curtailed by a sharp smack. Grenville's head snapped around. "I've heard that before, what is it?"

Pitiful tears were followed by a shrill shriek and then louder sobbing as a woman begged for mercy.

The man shook his head. "T'ain't right how he torments them. If I wasn't afeard for my life, I'd …"

"Who torments who?"

He gestured with the poker. "The chief. Or as he prefers, the master. Most of us call him the swine and, if you value your life, you won't be here when he's finished his rounds." Evil laughter swarmed up the tunnel, freezing them with its ferocity. "Which is now. He's looking forward to burning the truth out of this traitor." He pointed up to the cage, and Evadne struggled to maintain her composure. Now it had swung round, she could see the unconscious man was Kurt.

As Grenville pulled her away, she saw the sense in regrouping to formulate a plan, and they hid in a dark recess, unable to see, but hearing every sickening sound. The foul-mouthed monster nagged his subordinate to "haul the pathetic prick down a few feet so we can pick the best spot for my irons to sear his tender flesh." Something about the voice rang a bell.

A whispered huddle cooked up a plan requiring all three of them to screw their courage to the sticking place in order not to fail. Evadne wasn't sure whether she could pull off her part, but an unaccustomed faith in human nature had her praying the glimpse they'd seen of the burly assistant's humanity showed his softer side. If appealing to his better nature didn't work, she could take a leaf out of Rosalina's book and use feminine wiles – *whatever they were*.

But the nature of this particular beast would always be spanner in the works. A ruddy-great rusty iron one.

With Rosalina on his arm, Grenville adopted an officious air, striding in, his speech about being promised a private tour of the dungeons all prepared. But he barely got a word out before a familiar oily voice exclaimed.

"There you are! I was just on my way with a search party." *The jester? But how?* "You may as well join the fun, Evadne, I know you're there somewhere."

Seeing no reason not to, she complied, scanning around for the monstrous torturer.

"Looking for me?" The horrible voice sneered, and several jigsaw puzzle pieces in her mind assembled, waiting for her to work through the necessary clues so they could approach and couple with their correct neighbours. But some fog kept them apart.

"Question too difficult?" Back to the smug jester.

Her one working brain cell gave it a go. "You're the nasty gaoler?"

A scoff. "So, so limited. Your brain, that is. Try again."

"You're *all* the nasty evil apparitions."

A surprised pout. "Not quite so green as you're cabbage-looking."

Grenville gasped. "The crone in the greenhouse."

"Who's been keeping you in the dark and feeding you bullshit, Mr Mushroom." An ugly titter. "Not the hardest of tasks in my repertoire. *She*, on the other hand," he gestured at Rosalina, "got a little too close for comfort. On several occasions." A dark scowl bounced off as she folded her arms to deflect its power.

"Why? I hear you ask." He cupped his ear expectantly, but none of them would give him the satisfaction. "Or not. It would have been good to have you dance to my tune one last time, but no matter. The score currently stands at jester: thirteen thousand and fifty seven; team Sherlock: diddly squat. Sounds good to me."

With an eye-roll, Evadne side-stepped to pass him. He echoed her move, twice more before she desisted, folding her arms, barely managing not to tap her foot. "Go on then, have your Machiavellian gloat, but don't expect a gratifying reaction."

"We'll see. Would you really have offered yourself to the monster to free Kurt?"

What the what? Bugger. She clamped her eyebrow muscles, scolding them for being such easy marks, even as her two companions put themselves in dire danger of permanently shocked faces if the wind changed.

He capered around in triumph. "Easy marks all three." His face fell. "A moment ago you would have abandoned him, with no care for his health – or fate. Typical of the selfish bitch everybody knows and hates." The jester pulled no punches. "This is all your fault." He gestured at the inert Kurt. "That noble hero has been your right – and left-hand – man for years and you treat him like dirt."

Her hand went to her throat and she shook her head.

"Do you deny that you get all the kudos as the so-called talent? Not to mention the lion's share of the dosh?"

A shrug. "That's down to the TV company. They have rules about these things."

"So you didn't strike a deal to ensure he's never seen on screen, reducing him to just a backroom-boy salary? Did you know he gets no more than cameramen?" A beat. "Of course you did. No wonder he's bitter and twisted enough to cook up this scheme to pay you back."

Evadne gasped.

"And I leapt at the chance to help him torment the first class cow who treats ghosts – and anyone else with the misfortune to have dealings with her – with such disdain."

At least three of the puzzle pieces sidled up to be in spitting distance of making a solid corner, but their progress was halted by the cage swinging as Kurt stirred.

"It'll all come out now. How he came up with all these nefarious schemes to torment and cuckold you."

"How did you do it without your bosses finding out?"

"They're used to me dealing with external units – I'm their most experienced project manager in the area."

"You showed me the clause in the contract stipulating

the restrictions …" She broke off at his creamy-cat smirk.

"Kurt said you'd never read the original agreement, if you had it would've been a first. And being management it was no problem to doctor the file and substitute a copy. If you knew how often he'd forged your signature…"

Shaking his head violently, Kurt reached through the bars. "Eva, I would never–"

She cringed back. "Do you really hate me so much?"

"No, Eva. I did it because I love you. I only agreed to join in with his scheme when he taunted about you saying I was too tame and boring. You like your men dark and dangerous, so I tried to be like that."

She shrank back. "But to do all those dreadful things – or rather, to have all those dreadful things done to me."

"I didn't." He reached out again. "For the love of Christ, will someone get me out of here, please?"

Evadne's brain went into a meltdown, and she covered her face with her hands as all the puzzle pieces got whacked out of kilter and had to start again. Noises in the background suggested Rosalina and Grenville were helping Kurt out of the cage. Her over-riding feeling was her despair when Kurt tumbled over the battlements. This finally brought some clarity, as all four corners clicked into place and the edge pieces fell neatly between them like a choreographed dance routine. *A rumba, obviously*.

She opened her eyes to see him down on one knee, hands clasped, pleading.

"Forgive me, mein liebchen. When he roped me in, I never imagined the lengths he would go to, honestly."

She scoffed. "That's because you never met him, even

after you replaced him."

"You mean this is ..." He gasped.

"Nasty Nigel, the one who filmed the original pilot." She peeked at pompous git whose visible deflation had him growing a couple of inches in height as he lost the hunched back and ripped off the prosthetic mask at least as good as Robin Williams' character in *Mrs Doubtfire*. "I see you've learned a lot about character acting at the Castle. But it was Alton Towers I gave you the glowing reference for."

A slight incline acknowledged it. "Same company. But small recompense for what I could have had if only you'd been prepared to run with my idea. It had the potential for making us into TV legends. You cost me a glittering career with fame, fortune and lucrative book deals. The works."

"An on-again, off-again screen romance between co-presenters? I don't think anyone would have believed it."

"Because I'm not leading-man material?"

"Because I'm nobody's idea of a female lead."

The bald statement took any remaining wind out of his sails, but his twisted sneer aimed pure poison at Kurt. "You're welcome to the frigid bitch; she was the worst lay I've ever endured. I've warmer ice packs in my freezer."

Grenville's observation addressed nobody in particular. "Why do inept lovers always use the frigid accusation? I should do a study on it. And it's perfectly clear she would never lie with you even to prevent hypothermia."

"If that's the sort of man who turns you on, I see where I've been going wrong." Kurt's hands implored. "It's not who I am deep down, but I can certainly play the villain if you want me to."

"Don't be a silly sausage. He was right about one thing, I'd have done anything to save you." Kneeling down on the filthy floor, she treated him to the kiss of salvation.

~*~

"Th – th – th – that's all folks!" Kev had been waiting to use the phrase. As he copied Jen's trick of snapping the folder shut, he was gratified by the satisfaction on three of his players' faces and counted the studied neutrality on the other as a win. They were all happy to carry out the post mortem over dinner – another Wagamama extravaganza, but this time, Kurt insisted on paying in appreciation of being able to play the hero for once – and get the girl.

Georgie gave him kudos for getting an actual dragon and an actual dungeon into successive scenes. He lost a ton of brownie points and gained several chucked cushions when he admitted the riddle was a total red herring. "I had a few candidates depending on how quickly you solved it."

Later, Kev cornered Ben, asking for his real opinion.

"Honestly, pretty much what I said – I was expecting much more gratuitous sex and violence, but it actually turned out to be a sweet love story. *Who knew?*"

"You weren't sore about Isaac getting the girl?" A wink.

"Firstly, it was Kurt, not Isaac, and secondly, it's just a game – there's no way that's happening for real."

Kev's expression said "really?" while his mouth said, "watch this space."

Ch 19 – Full-on Mata-Hari

July 2022

As she stitched the last square into the baby blanket, Jen couldn't imagine where the time had gone. Teasing it into something approaching a rectangle, she spotted places where her tension had tightened – not enough to redo, but it made for interesting texture. Ah, what the heck – it would keep Timmy junior warm no matter what. Reaching for the white wool, she started the first of three edging runs which would give it a more uniform look – "like somebody owned it" as her gran might say. Her cousin Ellie would be coming up tomorrow and they'd visit together to cut down on the disruption for poor Karen – having two under two was no mean feat.

When she picked Ellie up at the station, they had the best part of an hour to kill before the allotted time, so they had a Costa, sharing a decadent piece of carrot cake.

"We should get a piece for Karen, she loves them."

"And she's breastfeeding, so she can eat a whole one with impunity. Lucky thing." Jen winked.

"I bet she's glad to finally drop. I can't imagine trying to carry a baby in this heat, it must have been sheer hell."

"Which is why I've brought her an extra fan, they reckon it's getting even hotter tomorrow."

"Timmy mentioned they've set up a paddling pool in the conservatory, and the pair of them stay cool in there."

"Fabulous. I bet she'll be an early swimmer."

Ellie had brought Vickie's diary, and they went through the scrapbook with shared reverence.

"Thanks for these, you're a star." Jen hugged her.

"I thought it might make up for you missing it for the third year running. My mate said thanks very much for the tickets, she was thrilled to go."

"Um. would you mind not saying anything to the guys, please? They think I was with you and I don't want to tell them where I really was."

"You already asked me, remember? You said they might have questions about having Covid, which is fine, because I did have it a while ago." She sipped her coffee, her gaze speculative. "Do I get to find out where you actually went?" A wink.

Jen chuckled. "In the fullness of time. Maybe."

"The look on your face says you had fun, and that's all I really want to know. So, where are we on the baby-name?"

When everyone had gone to bed, with Ellie safely tucked up in the green guest room, Jen retrieved her gran's diary, turning to the relevant date. Her memory was faint, but the entries on several days mentioned a woman who's name she'd always read as Jan because of Vickie's handwriting. Re-reading, she recognised shared exploits from her time in 1955, but when she read them originally, she'd had no reason to suspect it was her.

After Isaac's speculation about the real reason her gran quit, Jen scrutinised the subsequent entries, spotting an oblique reference to her giving up tennis for health reasons. It rang vague bells, and she remembered being stumped when she read it previously. But now it made perfect sense, especially after Dora ended up wheelchair-bound.

Opening the scrapbook, she returned to the shot taken at the practice court after Vickie and Bob had played Sheila and Mark in an anything-but-serious mixed doubles set. Spotting something in the corner of the photo which could have been the skirt she'd worn, Jen peered closer, tugging it out of the triangular tab keeping it in place. Something dropped out and fluttered to the ground.

The small sheet of wafer-thin writing paper was folded and she opened it with trembling hands. Her gran's handwriting changed Jen into Jan and she read on.

Dear Jan,

I know you'll never read this, but I couldn't think of who else to tell, and you said to write down my thoughts and feelings to lessen their power over me.

I'm in such a quandary over what to do about my tennis career. My coach is pushing me even more to practice with Mark after all the fuss of us being seen out together, and him winning the boy's title. He thinks we'd make an unbeatable mixed doubles pairing.

But I'm not sure I want to keep pushing myself down the road all the American girls go down – messing around with their bodies and missing periods and having to make themselves sick or worse if they eat a piece of cake. And I do love cake.

After the scare of Mum's osteoporosis, I've decided I want to study enough to at least keep myself healthy, and see where it leads. I used to wish I could be more like Daisy Greville, but now I wish I could be more like you – I'm sure you'd never let men boss you about.

She hadn't signed it.

Folding it twice, Jen held it to her heart, and whispered, "God bless you, Vickie" as tears started to flow.

That night saw her first decent sleep in a while, and she woke up renewed. Something had happened to make her brain glitch, and Ben and Georgie were the key. She had vague memories of them discussing her trip to the past, and they mentioned something peculiar. After dinner that night, when Isaac and Kev went off to continue their game, she confronted them. "Explain about Stepford-Jen."

"What if it sets you off glitching again?"

"I thought about that. You know yesterday when you and Georgie went into a weird military debrief routine? It's like you snuck round the … I'm gonna say *programming* in my brain. Then when Kev came in and was all Kev-like, it glitched again."

"Okay. So do what you must to return to that scenario and my colleague and I will continue our debrief."

"Sir, yessir." She saluted.

"At ease, soldier. Programming is an interesting word choice. Do you mean as in the sort of hypnotism techniques Woody Harrelson uses in the *Now You See Me* movies?"

"The 'get the quarterback' scene?" Georgie added.

"You got it. It's like a tiny part of me is watching this other me but *I* can't break through. I suspect it's how schizophrenics must feel."

"Bloody hell, Jen, this is not funny anymore. If he's playing mind games with you–"

"Who Isaac? He mentioned something about planting a few cues to ensure I got to the right place because he noticed disorientation after a couple of his trips."

"So he *has* been travelling. I *knew* it." Ben visibly clamped down on his natural reactions, trying to get back into character.

Somehow, Jen knew it wasn't necessary. "We can drop the debrief thing, the real me is in charge, however temporarily. And Isaac would never allow anyone else to have a go unless he'd thoroughly tested it out himself."

Ben's eyes narrowed. "He said that?"

"More or less. He's still trying to figure a lot of the details out."

"So why doesn't he talk to us about it?"

"Something about the power of thought. He reckons time-travelling is tied to deep-seated instincts, and too much information will skew the results."

"He's playing a dangerous game, Jen. So many things could go wrong." He explained how something as innocuous as leaving a letter had led to him and Georgie returning to an alternate 2022.

She sniggered. "Stepford-Jen sounds fun. A bit like Buffy-bot." She made like a robot. "I can do shiny-happy."

Although she laughed, concern tinted Georgie's face.

Jen patted her arm. "Honest, sweetie. This is just minor glitch – pun intended. And I think I've seen glimpses of Zac when Isaac was charming my gran and her mum." A grin. "See? I've stopped calling her Vickie, although it was wonderful to know her as a young woman. We should all get to take holidays in our ancestors' younger lives."

"Is that what he called it? A holiday in the past? I'm even more worried about the potential for paradoxes."

"I don't understand what he hopes to gain by not asking about our experience. From what you've said, he *must* know we went to 1977 – why bother to pretend otherwise?"

"It makes no sense to me either – unless …."

"What?" They both glared.

Georgie coughed. "Unless the jaunts have affected his health and he doesn't want to admit it."

"What makes you say that?"

"I know nosebleeds are the classic symptom for any kind of paranormal or psychic activity, but have you noticed the way he's always sniffing?"

"Now you mention it, I have." Ben frowned. "Whatever his reason, we need more info before approaching him."

"Why?"

"Because until we know how he's doing this programming stuff, he could do a mind wipe at any time."

Georgie scoffed. "I think you watch entirely too many espionage movies, but go on, what's the idea?"

"One of us needs to get past his OTT security."

"So you need someone to go full-on Mata Hari, and given him and Georgie will never be kissing cousins, it has to be me." Jen clapped her hands. "A new mission."

They gazed at her anxiously and she hugged them both. "Don't worry, I'm not glitching. This is me, Jen Paulson, saying 'bring it'."

"You'll have to be careful – he's not daft, and we don't know where Kev stands on this."

"Well that's easy. Georgie can distract him."

Ben chuckled. "Game on, ladies."

Dear Reader,

Thank you so much for reading this story – I hope you enjoyed reading it as much as I enjoyed writing it.

If you did, I'd really appreciate if you could let others know what was good/bad about it by leaving a comment on Amazon: *https://geni.us/TTjusttime*

Thank you

Jacky Gray

To find out more about my books, subscribe to my newsletter: *https://eepurl.com/b5ZScH*

Also by Jacky Gray

Time Doctors – Time-Travel meets Dungeons & Dragons
Time and Time Again
Just in Time
Time Kicks Back – Coming 2023

Calamity chicks 70s Sweethearts
Tina's Torment – Ugly Duckling
Chloe's Chaos – Goldilocks
Linda's Lament – Reluctant Rockstar

Bryant Rockwell – YA Contemporary Romance
New Kid in Town
The Show Must Go On
Leader of the Pack
Edge of the Blade
Music was my First Love
Stand by Me

Indivisible – BR Boxset #1-3
Invincible – BR Boxset #4-6

If you like historical-*ish* stories, Archer's magical world is now a 13-book saga featuring 3 different series:

Nature's Tribe – *Medieval Fantasy Saga*
3 Handfastings and a Burial – Wedding-themed shorts
12 Days of Yule – A Christmas-themed romance
8 Sabbats of the Year – A seasonal-themed romance
13 Esbats of the Moon – Dystopian origin story
Nature's Tribe Boxset – Books 1-4+Bonus short story

Hengist – *Medieval-alternate-world Fantasy*
Archer – A sensitive warrior
Rory – A lonely misfit
Reagan – An intrepid geek
Slater – A courageous time-traveller
Geraint – A reluctant heir
Archer's Quest – Books 1-2+Bad Boys
Uniting the Tribes – Books 3-5+Good Guys

Colour of Light – *the final series in the Hengist saga.*
Context – Short stories of rebellion & redemption
Chrysalis – Medieval magic meets modern-day mystery
Captive – Modern-day mystery meets medieval magic
Catalyst – Medieval magic meets modern military thriller
Colour of Light Boxset – Books 1-4+Bonus short story

Acknowledgments

Huge thanks to all the people who have supported me with constructive comments and suggestions. Special thanks to Paul for his technical expertise, and Katy and Andrea for adding polish and sparkle – really couldn't do this without you wonderful people brightening my days. Big shout out to the fabulous GetCovers designers for the awesome cover. And thanks to all those from Keith's awesome Broadhall Club who have helped out: Tracy, Georgie and Vickie, who all get starring roles. A big apology to my family who have suffered the sight of me chained to my lap-top for many more hours than they ought to have endured. But the biggest thanks go to all my readers – especially those who put a review on Amazon. *Thank You*.

About the Author

Jacky Gray's first career was telecoms and after 23 years writing software, she spent 17 years teaching kids, occasionally introducing them to the joy of maths. Teaching is now ancient history – a bit like the books she writes. Well, most of them.

Jacky lives in the English Midlands with her husband and the youngest of three grown-up children. She enjoys all live entertainment, watches a lot of movies and some great TV shows like GoT, Merlin, Robin Hood, and anything remotely Marvel. She listens to a lot of Journey and Queen and reads (apologies to the adverb police) voraciously.

About the Story

This was pure joy from start to finish. What's not to like about spending time in a majestic castle haunted by such disparate characters. Having visited it on several occasions, it was fun digging deeper into their sorry tales. Any resemblance to people who think they know me is pure coincidence – I borrowed some of your story, not your life.

Printed in Great Britain
by Amazon